Tattooed Memory

Abdelkébir Khatibi

Tattooed Memory

Translated by Peter Thompson

Authorized by Amina El Alaoui Khatibi

ISBN : 978-2-343-09724-4
EAN : 9782343097244

Reading Khatibi

Having now this *Tattooed Memory* in English reminds us of the store of Khatibi's (and the Maghrebi?) memory—of all its sources and his Moroccan childhood. But it also reminds us of our language and our languages, and that they (say, the original, French, version of this book) are not just the end point but also the source. In this case the sources are Berber, Arabic, and French. And a new end point (a source for the translator) is English.

Perhaps the deepest source is Berber culture. Childhood, mother, argan scents, tattoos on hands. And language. With all the other sources of this difficult poetry, we must remember that Arabic, French, Koranic ones come later.

The strain and discovery that marks writing/thinking in (at least) two languages throughout this narration produces the special trait of Khatibi's style. But the strain and discovery are also his content, his subject. This has been commented by many, but English readers have never been able to see its development (development through the growth of the self) as we do in Khatibi's first novel.

If there is another that urgently needs to be translated it is *La Blessure du nom propre*. It is here that language issues, Maghrebin struggles, and—once again, in Khatibi's innovative way—identity questions reach their fullest expression.

If there were a translator to take on this project, would that it be a poet-practitioner as honest and sympathetic as one Peter Thompson. ~~

Nabile Farès, winner, Kateb Yacine Prize, Lifetime Work

TRANSLATOR'S NOTE

This translation has been long in coming—perhaps, we imagine, because of its difficulty. One of the challenges came—in Morocco—in securing rights after Khatibi's death. The only other novel in translation is Richard Howard's version of *Amour bilingue* of twenty-five years ago.

Now, Gentle Reader, it is time to get down to what a friend of ours has called "brass tactics." This is a translation that "reads like a translation," and it does so because it is meant to. That is because the original reads like a translation. Or, to be exact about it, the original reads in Khatibi's unique "*bilangue*." This is a word, different from the adjective "bilingue" (bilingual) which Khatibi invented to explain what language was doing to him. Or to explain the odd sound of his written language and the way it reflects (putting it very briefly) conflicted interior idioms—especially in the novels (and most of all in this novel).

There is much to be said about identity, post-colonial ontology, "the language question"—and much has been very carefully said by Khatibi and others about his *bilangue* in this context. It is not easy to keep this discussion simple, especially when *Tattooed Memory* employs this linguistic trait along with all the different registers that meant so much to Khatibi: parable, Koranic reference, Berber language and folklore, Arabic, and references to calligraphy and to the Christian West. We add to that a specific theme, the tattoos—permanent Berber tattoos, or the temporary designs, usually on the hands, worked in henna—which serve as memories, preservers of culture, codes. A special pleasure is the polyvalence of this book's title: we think both of memory which bears a tattoo, and of memory that is itself tattooed onto a surface.

Conveying all this is a doubled language, one that never relaxes into a complacent *mono-langue*, but which instead seems uncomfortable in its own skin. The most important consideration is that, for Khatibi, the situation is positive. He has spoken positively—somewhat the way Chinua Achebe does—of the tension between the colonial language and the mother tongue. Césaire, Senghor and others have found that writing in the colonial language has some positive features and that, at the very least, their inward tension is rich and stimulating. The difference is that the settled idiom of their writing (except for some of Césaire's poetry) doesn't show the tension as Khatibi's *bi-langue* does. A closer analogue might be Amos Tutuola, whose *The Palm-Wine Drinkard* is a linguisitic experiment that blends two languages in a continuously startling way. His subject, though, stands apart as a series of magical vignettes that (in part) mimic African folk traditions. Khatibi, by contrast, uses a language that suggests discomfort, strain—in some ways Frantz Fanon's "nervous condition" of the colonial subject. And the tension—not always a negative element—is doubly effective because *Tattooed Memory* is part bildungsroman (even exploring life outside Africa at times) and pursues an investigation of problematic identity, linguistic and otherwise.

The translator, then, has to step back and see if the strange vocabulary, neologisms, awkward syntax and sudden changes of rhythm and register have come through in the English. Quite often they have, for reasons that are easy to imagine. Sometimes things need to be tweaked, in a direction that reverses the translator's usual efforts.

Everyone's ideal, for some reason, is a "smooth" translation. Here that ambition would be illegitimate.

We have avoided footnotes. Notes by Khatibi clarified that "St. Phallus" alludes to the artist Niki de Saint Phalle, and that the magnificent Sartre which the narrator has "in his hands" is *Existentialism Is A Humanism*. I note that the first poetry citation is from Baudelaire, and the second ("…and I've read all the books") is from Mallarmé.

I am greatly indebted to Fatma Ghailan, who offered very substantial help in a number of areas. The Provost's Foundation to Promote Scholarship and Teaching at Roger Williams University provided an invaluable course release. And Mme. Amina El Alaoui Khatibi, was especially generous. The translation is dedicated to the memory of my father, Cameron Thompson.

Rabat, May, 2016

Long have I guarded the sacred ritual of my birth. They put a little honey on my lips, a drop of lemon on my eyes, the first gesture to free my gaze toward the universe and the second to invigorate my mind, to die, to live, die, live, doubled upon my double—what, was I born blind to myself?

I was born at the Aid el Kebir festival; my name suggests a thousand-year rite, and it happens now and again that I imagine Abraham cutting open his son. There's nothing to be done—even if the song of throat-slitting doesn't obsess me—there is still, at the root of it all, the name's rending; from maternal violins to my own will power, time remains fascinated with childhood, as if writing, by giving me to the world, replayed the shock of my bursting forth, in the fold of a dark doubling. Nothing to be done, my soul takes to eternity.

My name keeps me at the moment of birth, between God's scent and the starry rhythm of signs. I am a servant and I reel; my self deleted through images, I align with that question of mine that wanders among letters. There isn't a green blade, nor a dried up one, that can't be found in plain writing!

Tattooed Memory

I was born with the second war, so I grew up in its shadow and few memories come back to me from that time. Adrift in my recall are vague words about the scarcity of goods or the drama of parents brought together willingly or by force. Radio Berlin seized our fathers' attention; international history entered my first years through the voice of the sinister dictator.

Expeditions, during air raids, in a vacant lot by the sea. We left behind a city completely extinguished; pillage and theft were king. In the street I made myself gobble the bread I was supposed to bring home from the shared oven. I got home with my legs strained and tense. Poor country people, fleeing the nearby plain, crossed through the neighborhood in a whirlwind of violence. Other lives, much the same, drag through that past. Long after, when I tried to transcribe that misery, I could only do it through a shrill disorder of my whole body, barb-wired into the most extreme uncertainty. Was I dreaming paradise? Rivers of honey flowed nowhere in the irradiation of my little illusions; I was the son of him who begat my father, a child in whom his tribe withered, in a genealogy more and more broken. And now I think my profession—this divided gaze toward others—takes root in the off-chance, in the lure of finding myself again, beyond this humiliated group who were my first people.

During the sirens I stayed late to slip among the ghosts, at the edge of the rocky square, while the men prayed, a trembling huddle whose fear drifted as an echo in my own ravings. Nothing erases these wanderings on the beach but the mad rain, falling through my drowsiness, while the leaning voice of my grandmother recited, at night, new heights of stridency. Tumble, grandmother!

15

Other people's war went by quickly, like a far and imaginary combat, without corpses, without tangible blood, a combat with invisible adversaries ending with episodes that at first seemed funny. Fuck fuck lady, the Americans asked while handing out gum. With them I learned the way to the whorehouse. The town's prostitutes were amused, I was told, by these stubborn chewers who hid their members in little baggies no one had ever seen before.

The labyrinth grew more challenging for these Americans, looking to fornicate. On their approach everyone in the neighborhood disappeared. The Americans stormed about, raging madmen. I caught them threatening my father with their weapons—my father, who, not knowing what they wanted from him, was trying to get away. He succeeded, now left to his terror. No-Luck, the famous hoodlum of the quarter, defended our honor. What would my father have done if the soldiers had broken down our door and raped my mother? This fantasy was ever with me.

No-Luck divided his time between jail and the street, his flabby form blurred in space, beating the air with his tattooed hands. This crook, fascinating to us kids, smashed the obstacles of the street, slamming into the walls with his swaying shoulders. He stank, grunted, gave the pavement a confused look.

In reconstituting itself, the portrait of this hoodlum, surging back with doubled strength through my sexuality, now sends me back to the sophistication of people—or characters—of old predictions, as if desire, never exhausted in abstinence, can only fixate on the flowers of another language entirely, before the frustrated joy of my body rushes forth.

The same fascination before every tattooed Bedouin woman. When she unfolds her ancestral hand I wed my

16

fixation on myth. Any calligraphy distances death from my desire, and tattooing has the exceptional privilege of preserving me. No trap door into chaos, only the force of an unleashed impulse, a graph quick as an eye-blink.

No settling of accounts with my parents. I wish to massacre neither father nor mother. I was born at the beginning of the war and my father died just after it ended; not enough time to know each other, observe his life on the rebound, reap a complete cycle where a haggard era frays. My mother lets me be, but we share a dream—she will go to Mecca even if my god is dead.

I recognize the liveliness of her old look when she tells me about my suffering, my weaning at eighteen months. My older brother "stole" the breast of his sleeping mother. They made him swallow a mouse fried in butter. Nice way to punish incest! "The small bones for me!" my brother announced. And for me, a few fragment of the Koran copied onto a cookie. All returned to the path of paradise, though after that my mother's nipple was bitter.

The French who colonized us, explained my mother, resemble, here at the point of Independence, children removed from their mother's breast. For her mother, only this separation could explain the madness of our attackers. Born in the dust of the French landing at Casablanca, she once saw me, later on, hands-up before a paratrooper's machine gun. I was taken with my brothers to parts unknown. My mother wept, as the matter remained opaque and began to drift, out there, in a steady beat of pain and torture. Did my sweet mother think she was the Nymph Calypso, the all-powerful with winged words who locked Ulysses in her four-fountained cave? Their separation a wondrous tale: as departure approached, the godly hero, they say, dried his tears. Their last night unfolded in nectar and ambrosia.

17

The mythic freshness of this meeting with the Occident leads me back to the old wavering image of the Other, a contradiction of aggression and love. As an adolescent I wanted to define myself in a nostalgic harkening to the founding myth.

A bad attack of trachoma after weaning. Visit, with my mother, to the healing *marabout*. We were asleep in his sanctuary when she had the following dream: she sees herself in our house; the light is on, even though it is day. Masons are toiling. Then she sees the *marabout* offer her a fig, she takes it and asks for another. Her wish is granted. She says to me, "The figs are your eyes." The next morning they dropped egg white in my eyes and declared me cured. What could I say, it was true! Ah well! There's no cure that isn't a text.

I remember this suffering well, and so many colors stolen from my illness. I loved to stare for a long time at the hottest face of the sun. Was it my timid questioning of the world's great silence? My gaze, in love with grasshoppers, roamed in religious imaginings. The seven paradises and the infernos, God and Satan, the prophets and humanity young again, man eternally beautiful and wise, the promised *houris* at last, soaring above after death, life and death. I unfastened myself from the sun, briefly damaged, and already felt sad and old. At these moments time spread in all its burning, and I riddled myself about my flight. Really! Life is nothing but this clamping off of time which coils in a limitless spiral? Far from being happiness run through with cracks, this was a mirror whose reflections I put together, but as the projection of a child beyond all signs.

The weirdest image of my father is somehow comic: walking in the street, he is rigid, from sky to earth, crushing me with his height, and me trotting along silent. I was happy. The only photo I have kept of him offers me the face of a jailbird, head bare, hair cropped, ears pointy, the gaze an acid sweetness, and some faded fingerprints below.

Rigidity in the face of my mother's jovial curves, a dry fig and medicinal at that, whose coupling I couldn't imagine. In this couple, whose intimate life was the secret of the gods, I see as separate parallels an irresistible tenderness and a goat's assault—my father. From these depths I was born.

My father passed his life between God and money; often he put them in one pocket. Theologian, arid inspirer to the true path, he stood up to the venality of the Muslim judges. Graying preacher, gifted businessman, he lived a fierce and morose duality. Normally he dwelled in the Koran, surrounded by his family or his acolytes, a large brotherhood—slept late among his books, awoke with a shock in the wee hours. Once retired to the second floor, God watched over our sleep. A fleeting protection when I awoke. God has left for the day; after that I went to try to sneak a vague tenderness, over the top of his glasses. And then, in his moments of anger, there was that barrel where I submerged myself, teeth chattering.

Had he discovered history without my knowing? Neither reformist nor mad for power, he was a conspirator with no plot, yet refusing to yield. Had he understood that there was nothing to learn from the West, because his God was a living one? His poor head evinced the sadness of those who get themselves expelled, in a dispossession ever more mutilating.

19

This man who hardly touched my mother hurled himself at the eldest son. I came along in third position: my father agreed to send me off to the French-Moroccan school—I became a consciousness of demotion, and one abandoned to impiety. Orphan of an absent father and two mothers, would I pick up the tick of always alternating? And can it be written, the portrait of a child? Because the past that I now choose (as a kind of motif for the tension between my being and its evanescences) settles itself according to my incantatory celebration, itself a pretext for a violence that I dream to the point of madness, or of some other self-absorbed idea. Who can write his own silence, memory's slightest deletion?

Who can recite my past in the erasure of a page, who might vary the darkness merely by pulling off wings? More than just my will, look, here is my plaintive memory, here it is, freed from its face! An ivy vine's trace that doesn't betray the child I was, the fertile child not yet dead in me!

I just had a slip: mother, instead of memory—double absence in a double fluke. Making a childhood—nothing will close this idea of transcription.

Perhaps this fear of a certain past is the inversion of my brutal discovery of death. My little brother abandoned me and became a bird of paradise. After his death, my mother protected him from the flames of hell, suffering in silence; not a tear to mar his happiness, never again! Dying as a little boy, as tradition has it, is an inner dawn that veils every chaos, and we reinvent the ecstasy of the womb. And this little brother left me a key secret: using his toys I began again the assembling of our past, the first theater where, with fragile eyes, I interacted with a corpse.

At age seven, death came into my life with such fury that I still feel the howlings racking me, writhings of someone thrown—tied hands and feet—into a mad identity. I carry within me the grating cry of three brothers given over to their shared derision. Age seven: the hour of realism!

By evaporating, my father became immemorial speech. So, for a child, dying, or coming apart through the father's absence—was there any difference? The body was ready—everything had been prepared, ordained, settled. I thrashed the staircase every which way, propped against the nearest indolence, then hung from the wall where my weeping slid. Endless parade of unknown faces; they wailed, savored their food, feast and murder drawn together in lugubrious chant. Before the white sheet scented with rose water stretched over the cadaver I was completely enigmatic to myself; between him and me, a love in ashes. The cortège in single file, all through the town, as the coffin advanced in its miserable majesty. It will be noted that I trotted after it, one step behind, two steps into the void... and above the cortège this breath of mercy, gliding.

Now at the cemetery, a vacant lot where dogs consort with wild grass and, in spring, daisies and shrubs. A hole must be found and then the trick is turned, beautiful, worth as much (and no more) as losing oneself in the posture of the holy man of the caves. In this lot, rain washes away the red earth, in the sun some graffiti stand out on my father's tomb. Here lies that icy rhetoric, at the heart of my childhood.

They handed out dried figs to the poor, I didn't have time to wish my father dead, even *a posteriori*. You have a mother, you'll say. Ah happiness! But a mother doesn't fill in the absence of the father, and I was his accomplice. Even demoted, even deviant, I prolonged the family tree, I was protected. My mother, my poor mother, I hardly knew her, I sidled by her on tip toes. She brought children into the world, the street lapped them up. I recall the street, more than I do my father, more than my mother, more than anything there is. Latent tenderness every time I come back to that street, the same disorientation as when I come home after a long absence. A few yards from the family house, all in a split second, the void invades me, memory vanishes, lightning flash of a definitive immobility. Nailed in place, I hesitate to move forward; color saves me on the spot, perhaps my preferred mauve. I have to—even keeping my eyes open and staring straight—keep on going, avoiding any suspicious moves, any stumbles, my weight glued to the weight of the load. This clamping on can happen, however, without any damage, the muscles' elasticity remaining unchanged. To regain my balance in the street, I can invent myself a pretext for confronting this brutal evasion, I can tell myself that it's good to find joy in rediscovering my family, talking to them, my caressing hand on their shoulders. If, all of a sudden, I no longer recognize the street, if my body floats free of its spatial coordinates, it's because I no longer know why I'm there, or what I came to do. No more movement toward the others, only a color, itself the mirror of my separation.

In time, I succeeded my father, my older brother—and his impossible image—and now dream of abolishing every tribe, of being a top-ranked wrestler...

Let us segue with a distant memory. Around the age of four, I was caught by high tide on a rocky little island at Essaouira. A long drift among the little creatures under rocks, a moment which moated me off from the world by enclosing me in an hour more and more entangled.

22

Abandoned, far from my playmates, I cast a last look ahead and, without a sound, I plunged on, fully dressed, and passed through the water; a little deeper and it would have choked me. I came home all water and sand, my aunt was beside herself.

In the depths of this scene the only childhood dream whose precision remains shows me rolled up in a great wave, then hurled onto the beach. No feeling of terror, rather a waiting, a void, as when after a shock you wait to catch your breath. Ocean, mother, memory—lapses fleeing from this chill nostalgia.

So decisive was the accord between the sea and my body that for a long time I was unaware of other marvels—the whiteness of snow, the forest, even the woods full of scents. An accord predestined, perhaps you'll think, since the sea is the motif for my first melody.

The men who colonized me, along with their children, seemed to live by the rhythm of the seasons, in a cosmic harmony that was almanached and transmitted over and over. Until the age of seventeen I had never seen either snow or a forest—not a true, deep one. The stuff of postcards or fairy tales: forests that trembled as one entered them, snow that fell on children on their way to school. Bah! Nothing really, a moment's reflection when I spoke, as an adolescent, of weeping willows whose shape I really didn't know, songs of birds I happily killed with a pitiless snare. I grabbed these birds, strangled or still dying. I went to ponder their bodies on our ever-airy terrace: the sea slipped away to the horizon.

While recently reading Gombrowicz's *Cosmos*, I recognized as my own the book's salient image: vision of a bird hung in the forest, where two paths meet. The killer is never named, because for one thing we are all linked to this suspended gesture, and also because the massacre of

23

birds, frenzy emerging through white words, signals my devout participation.

One day a bizarre giant with cauliflower ears carried of my maternal aunt—who was, in a sense, my real mother. Infinitely mocking, and at the very edge of the real, this man dragged legs like stilts, was easily miffed in the street and swelled himself with fake airs. A pointed tarboosh that aimed at the ever-changing path, one leg wandering and widely splayed, diphthong against all diphthongs, he proceeded. He had a wild laugh, and heard nothing but chance in the wind. They said, during my adolescence, that several times he staged his own hanging, with a feeble rope. He screamed falsely, let his own suicide go wrong so miserably that we laughed out loud. He reaped only our pity.

Abduction of my mother in her fourth month of widowhood by a ratty man who was crushed under our contempt. Abduction, as well, of my aunt who took me away with her to Essaouira. I gave no trouble on this first love voyage *à trois*. They coddled me, made my life easy, I was happy.

Surrounded by a harem of seven little Berber girls—a paradise about to be lost—I picked up the rudiments of the game of eros. This was a balance sheet already weighed down by a child dissociated from the family, shy and fearful, who amused himself—to satisfy his reveries— gazing straight into the sun.

I was already familiar with the terrorism of fathers, I had lived with mine as if in a shadow play, each to his own role and God help the hindmost. I learned, as you're supposed to, the rites of respect and the commandments, the code of a godly family. A bit older, I conquered the

24

space around me with tiny steps, but I tumbled back into fatigue and evasion, with solutions impossible and my return defeated. The circle soon closed on my rebellions against my father and that maternal silence.

This abduction shuffled all the cards. My aunt had protected me, keeping me to one side in my own family. Son of a parallel mother, I plunged straight into the encroaching of identities, duplicity, and belonging to a kind of poisoned happiness. With my aunt's marriage I became, at four years old, the precocious spectator of a girl's rape.

My aunt bore herself like a feather, fingers drawn out like fleshless velvet, going through the motions without joy; everything stayed still, she glided between walls. In her presence, though, a drowsy tenderness, the slapping of a wave. At night, I thought of the sudden flesh of her husband. A doubled incest is the dream of many children, and in my case a dream against an unnatural father, my uncle.

The woman amused herself nibbling along the surface of the walls, and advanced in the household, in spite of herself, with the coldness of a conspirator overthrown. Single, she surrounded me with her affection; now that she was married she forgot about me. I lost, forever, my carefree ways, and I was taught that you don't kill traitors. And just then a beggar came into my aunt's house with a hidden gift. We opened her basket: a sleeping baby. Was there any way to behold her without annihilating myself? There was nothing more for me there, despite my harem; I stalked around my replacement in a limping solitude. Another girl! So the maternal reign went on...

Playing adult saved me from boredom: my loving cohabitation with a young maid, same room, sometimes the same bed. She violated me—I was four.

25

She would wake me up and initiate me every which way, cushions here, remains of my slumber there, and always the softness of great dizziness. I still have before me the image of that girl, reduced to begging an impossible orgasm, her frenzied abandonment in a child. And then?

When I went back a year later to my real family I was drawn to these precocious delights with another maid. This time, I was able to get hard. We used to sleep, she and my two brothers, in the same room—which became a place of orgies. This maid became our brothel, and we— we partook, in the night's trembling, of a tribal pleasure. At that age when I became erect I didn't feel, unless my memory is tricking me, this almost suffocating burning in the loins, just before great pleasure; then, it was a tender tickling of the penis, a delicate tickling, always at the same degree of stimulation, a kind of monochord pleasure which was enjoyed over a low flame. I loved that woman, I loved the round warmth of her thighs when, drowsily, I clambered up on her belly. One time I fell asleep on her, an obstacle for my brothers—who had to shove me off. The older one must have had a draining time of it, since he was up at dawn for prayer. For me, it was sleeping late, then running off with a *beignet* in my hand and an even warmer memory in my cock.

I discovered brothels a bit later, around age nine. We went there in groups after school, and lined up single file: we headed for one whore who was completely nonjudgmental and whose strange name still grates in me. An old and easy-going woman, she casually welcomed what we had all chipped in. Fastidious puritan that I was, I was disgusted by her gravelly voice, her vulgarity and her bead-string of insults. Disgusted as well by her tobacco breath, and the yellow sex, plucked and prickly, that she wet with saliva. The same feeling as whenever my hand brushes a hedgehog: a shaved sex, erupted from the earth and about to bloody you. Disappear, grandmother!

The whores of Casablanca smoked cigarettes vaginally—nothing finer, of course! The brothel of our little town was modest: mercenary but artisanal, an intimate brothel, almost a family. Nowhere the mixed smells of tobacco, sperm, spices, and the aggressive scents of Spanish cologne. Whores caked with make-up, as usual, with the blood-streaked look of clowns. But this kaleidoscope that I could feel putting me to the test was really a banal subversion, and I could no longer count my fingers. Such was the piercing cry of thousands of whorehouses at the edge of my nightmares. As an adolescent, it was settled: let's snatch the dark's purity from the whore, and the heart's whoring from the pure maid. A dichotomy mystical in all aspects; I divided all others up among my specters, and classified myself in a strange eroticism. The same thing at that age—the temptation to be ready for anything at all, to be necessary, to leave behind a history or a personhood, to push destiny by force of ideas and generous acts. You have to laugh when shrewd biographers take that as a taste for eternity. As everywhere, the fog is thick, bare your chest and push on!

Look up at the flowers on the ceiling; I looked and my foreskin was off. The circumcision festival was just beginning, we went under the scissors, my brothers and I. Ow! Ow! Perhaps we will come to pardon those orange tree blooms—on these myrtles and this incense. Pray to your Lord! To the purest, the most honest one. Pray to your Lord! And he will turn against us, the day of The Great Misstep. Salt the foreskin and hurl it away! And now what! –the tribe of women, is it aflame too? They bear you now on a white sheet, and what a strange swap—their signs for my wound.

27

The world separates, becoming two, I float, an immemorial shriek, far beyond what was torn, an indefinite cry that will collapse my final cruelty; I float, though holding up because of the delightful warm chicken between my teeth, I float in a fugue of spices, not alone, with three brothers, three foreskins gone; the same as the scriptural expulsion, deriving all things: seeing what, as the pair of scissors appears, crying in the void and farther and farther, gaze scribed ever after on the fake flowers. My father hiding in his bedroom, he wouldn't see me, I gesticulate for everyone: what trophy will be yours, father, as you stoop to flee? You weep, perhaps, in a corner while I howl through my father's breath. Say it: Allah is great! Say again: we will have ablutions of blood and love. Then the transposition of spice into color, it is there that the memory stuck, more than any fleeting sensation in my body; perhaps they feasted better having offered me up to the women; to all of them I owe this wound. I discern a vague plot to have me kneel; meanwhile, they make me come down the stairs that I've bounded up alone practically since birth. They hoist me on a crowd of celebrating arms, they shout victory. At first I faint dead away. My mother's shout wail wakes me. She goes through the motions of putting me to bed again, and she weeps; I am split upon the enigma of women: on the celebrants some rose water to sprinkle, my eye takes a bite, everything fades out. And it's not the death of the innocent. Don't you believe you've been raised in the dignity of the patriarch? Be worthy of your blood, be a patriarch! Marry one, two, three, four women, and get on with it! Inherit, little one, inherit from your father, from your father—this crack won't kill you. Those who have erections, when they're not circumcised, know only torment and annoyance! The ones of The Great Misstep! Know this, propitious one, know well! You may be able to

28

launch yourself as parable. And why not! Huff and puff against the pain! Separate yourself and move on! And walk, your knees apart, don't let it rub against your white clothes, be vigilant!

Now, for mobility, the opening of a blood flower, tattooed between your thighs.

As a child, I had killed off a species of sparrows; may the forest pardon me, it's yet another disorder of my fingers, one that makes me shiver. And so this beheaded rooster in our house: its head, in its writhing, offered a splendid dance, a line of scripture was all that was needed to slurp at the jugular vein, to let the feathers drift about, in the extreme reduction of a poem attributed to a master hand. But the rooster remained rooster and me, I didn't feel like dying.

Later, the haunting of the scissors tore at my member. I trembled openly, a side-step close to total loss—write it all and imagine everything, that was the code of my generation, that was the whole picture.

Through circumcision I acceded to gratitude, to a hairless manhood. My mother put a girl's henna on my hand, this pale reddish-yellow never transgressed against. Be a man! Be a woman! She took care of me and spoiled me, we played together, one, two, three, four, five and the grasshopper bounds, I soar with the swallow, I plunge with the eagle, remain alone, climb all alone, go back down all alone, rise again with everyone. I was happy, following the movement of my hands.

I had gone to the Koranic school for a while. They asked me to practice calligraphy, because it leads, the *fqih* always said, straight to paradise. To write on the wood plank you had to fashion a thin reed, dip it into a deep inkwell, and patiently recompose the Koranic parables until the images sang.

The little plank on which my knowledge was supposed to develop stayed white for long periods; I could neither write, nor sharpen the wooden pen; I rested the plank on my knees, like a pointless symbol. The *fqih,* a patriarch clearly close to God through his beard and his bearing, taught us a few mnemonic devices. My memory blossomed vaguely, then quickly became rotten fruit. Very early I got to know the failed act, the perception of a doubling of language. My time, then, to yell out no matter what for long hours, overwhelmed by the noise, under the contemptuous gaze of the patriarch. Days in linear time, reduced to a fixed space where the circle of children caged in their bodies closed in on a sadistic divinity. This patriarch, supported by the community, sometimes ate in front of us; we faced the wall while he nourished himself. Shouting against this wall I dreamed of fleeing. Unarmed, I held back tears, failure.

Before my father I bowed my back, bent myself to the role of complicitous slave. I avenged myself stealing money for my brothers or drawing cowboys on his desk, monolithic ones and dim, barely knowing how to grip their revolvers. None of this caused alarm, I went dragging on through my bored and docile life. The street got me, I snuck around that labyrinth where anything might jump out: wild cats, women's eyes in doorways or along the house-walls, *jnouns* behind the Barbary figs. I was there for the awful whippings on the sole of the foot, when the master's anger erupted. They held the victim down, he crumbled afterwards, a little drool on the reed mat. I took off at prayer time—they called me a hoodlum; I reclaimed the tactics of the street.

30

My archetypal childhood: I refresh my memory with the brief movement of a woman's hand when she pulls shut a patched up old door—would-be obstacle to rape. I run through my childhood in those little swirling streets, houses all unequal heights, labyrinth that shatters at the corner of one omen or another. But what is this thing, a street? This limestone foliage, worn off by rain. I cross through my childhood over these upturned tombstones, and if starving cats are collapsing in the sun, there is still finery coming from all directions, the breakthrough gained by a special theft, above all: this vacant lot—where rise the Barbary fig trees of my distant cry, *jnouns* and *houris* darting in the night, to top off the strangeness. I sang and threw stones.

One street attacks another, and there's the fear of bats too—their ridiculous and timorous erasures. With a shred of onion on a reed we chased those oily shapes, useless wings I abstained from wrecking—the night made little cuts in our feet. Let us pass on, for a moment, to the house, along this same path of parable. The father slept alone, on the top floor; the mother below, in her own room. Between them my cohabitation with brothers and maid. Deep in the paternal bedroom that grandiose wardrobe, with a streaked rectangular mirror, locked tight while it silted up before my eyes in an odor of mothballs, memory of the graveyard or of moths defeated a thousand times, who fluttered back to the rolled up documents, jewels, gaudy tissues or old banknotes—and behind it all—a ring with a little glass bead: Mecca!

The terraces linked easily. I stalked them all, my head bent over the courtyard of my choice. The bigamous neighbor complained to my family about my aerial

31

evasions. I was elusive. I controlled adults through the detachment of my own flights, a meager pleasure despite the competition with stray cats, with extremely complex soccer games—one step back and two steps into the void, later indeed will come suspense, danger's fable.

Hurling myself down the short stairway near the electric meter, I turn completely around, my wish sealed, my wish buried, I walk in a waking dream on the flagstones of a small room with a gaping doorway, across from our room whose only window said no; to the right the secret spot of obese rats, boisterous, with muzzles fit to plug all manner of excavations, should the night turn strange. There is also the kitchen, dark and black from smoke, there the exile of utensils hefted to the notes of a song; my mother sat facing the light.

My choice was to attack the bigamous neighbor, rigid, king in a non-speaking role, his concise wives in charge of every sudden word. I can't get rid of the striking image of each one. This duo offered both the beautiful and the cursed, the sterile and the breeder of children. Leaning over one side or the other, what was I to think? One wife sparkles now, given over to a French soldier, a chubby red-faced one. Because of all the pork and wine. Ah, so God fattens up the infidels the better to roast them? I refused to greet this good fellow. A Sunday for the French living in Algeria was a Sunday apart: tangos, grunting waltzes, a sweet stench, boozes too aggressive for my own excesses. Through the fanlight: the Western carousel of colonials with nothing to do.

Had I really tried to seduce that ample woman, with her drooping shoulders? Let's just say that I was beginning to go bad by little shiverings, each time I dared brush against

32

her bare shoulder. She was the mistress of our latent tenderness, that nostalgia for all women that my young gaze dreamed up. This way, ashes and dust!

As for him, the corner fqih endlessly married and divorced for a quarter of a century; each time, I was the age of his offspring: impossible to glide on my own wings toward his women, always beautiful and young. Protected by learning and his harem—which he rarely brought together in the same rhetoric—the patriarch entered the absolute. He said: Dry your eye, my child, they will cause fresh dates to rain down on you, and rivers of honey to flow, signs for such as thee who are gifted with wit. First the rod before your eyes to punish you, child, then the gift of women here on earth for those who are deserving. This gift is ephemeral, but necessary, child. If you doubt this, then marry them all! Quiet, quiet, quiet! And lo I bow my head when the patriarch prays, we stopped tearing the wings off flies since, smeared on the wall, and purple like little bits of spring, who had cried out?

I was growing fast though time was no longer the same, which didn't matter because now the sun was possible, thus I was told by the other old man of my childhood, surrounded by his green tea and loaves of sugar, his body decrepit, a few bubbles of fog drifting over his slow eyes, where old age hung for a broken down moment. The neighborhood lived in an advance wave of parables, and in the evening invitation to converse among the stars.

At home, when the house began to sketch a feminine conversation, I went along with those parallel cousins, the girls, for me it was some notion of blood stored up in a virginity from before birth. I achieved endogamous

33

balance: they served me, very matter-of-factly, a marriage of two marriages. They teased me about my green eyes.

No sobbing can contradict me, I appeal to the water's heat. In point of fact there won't be any defection by the Turkish bath or its mirrors. Therefore the door opens; my mother is already improvising in a screened light, she filters her clothes and mine with one sound. Enter the steam, clam belly! One eye leaps forth, another wanders, may they both be drawn in unto fire! I feel my way, here is the circle on the tiles, yours, a warm coin, a warmer one, a third—in short, echoing to a final vertigo, they're rubbing my chest, back, the rest becomes unreal, I approach the tub of boiling water and I'm afraid of falling, a woman brusquely parts her thighs unto infinity, a gaping transfixes me, and who cried out? Who fled, bounding over the tiles? I lost, in a flash, all those women of my childhood. I lost them, and, in a sense, I became, after this broken ternary order of things, the father of my mother, of my brothers, and of blind analogies...

I was born within the rhythm of my town, carried by the soft, salty wind of the Ocean. Open Thalassa's heart, you will see there the crossed root of a branch and a glance. This glance summons the renaissance of a space. Through the play of dissimulation a memory transforms the town of our past into a blank nostalgia; the pathways part and end up at the same knot, neighborhoods cross-reference in a jigsaw puzzle of shapes, surfaces, and colors. Two images stand out in my nomadic memory, light and mobile images like a swallow's geometry or the muffled appeal of desire. Kif's smoke, the sea singing in the whites of my eyes. Peace! Peace! Peace!

Two Parallel Towns

El Jadida.

Boy my age with head shaved bald, except for a long forelock in the middle of his skull indicating the direction of the wind, or of school. If you haven't had a forelock in the middle of your skull, you can't understand, obviously, what I might dare say about my own generation, the one of forelocks in fact, the last race, and now disappearing beneath bellies of an irresistible weight.

The barber collected foreskins and forelocks, operations officially connected, but which fork apart horribly. I knew some—barbers of caressing touch—who cut our hair accompanied by the trilling of canaries, a trilling added to the more public sounds, sounds that were sandy, impossible to pin down; as a small boy I harvested, haphazardly, a little blood on part of my skull. If ringworm was growing apace with spring the barber let his hesitant hand glide, and instead of giving in to temptation, he then went by it, acting as if nothing was up, scratching right near it. You will call it a revelation full-blossomed down to the stalk, forelock and wonder of the desert.

Quite another thing, being able to walk all around town. A few sagging four-wheeled barouches, horses so thin you wonder if they'll get through the day. Their driver acts about to hit them, grits his teeth, stands there a howls; the whip that bites with its own snap falls, invariably, on our heads, we who are sitting around. You have to deserve your walk around, we don't protest, the driver asks no more than that. He has a special tenderness for his animals, tenderness and various feelings no one denies. When one of the horses feels like stubbornly letting fly a liquid first yellow then rainbow, the barouche stops, it's a party. Believing, in the end, that horses just do anything that enters their heads, and perhaps being now more horse than his horses are, the driver no longer controls the situation. Alert to any plots, however, with every new day he watches over the transformation of urine into rainbow.

Anyway, gathered in the center of the town the horses go on a revolving strike, feign frightful headaches along with the kilometers of pee that cross the town; the road is straight, pedestrians from here know perfectly the detours, fantasies, the timetable of fantastic colors, everything.

Instructed by our little donkey at the water-wheel, I was patient. Because of this game: simple as it turns out, you wait until the horses move one hoof, then another, you freeze, then with a mad laugh or strange fit you send them careening off to their destiny.

The driver wants to be paid in advance, he's not trusting, well what do you expect! Money, money, money! He couldn't care less about anything else, out of respect for his animals, and also he knows everything, as you do when you let yourself be guided by this whip right-out-of-the -movies! God has spoken, and has not decreed, and yea even more, you look for the correct word, such is the second way out, otherwise we switch carriages and so on after that. Perhaps mercy will be shown us for this mobility, on the day that we dance, face turned to the sun.

The horses stop to eat, far off, or near. The heaps of hay do not satisfy their passion. They savor, naturally, the freshness of their colors, green grasses, purple figs, motley clothes of the peasant women... The townspeople grasp, by a sort of repeated divining, that the horse is not the enemy—but behind every plot, undeniably, there is the fly. Squatting or stretching itself on the eyes of this poor animal, the fly goes exactly where he goes, changes neighborhood and mood, goes back to the stable in the evening. To excite the horse, you have to excite the fly; to excite the fly, you have to stir up all the other flies, a vicious circle if it were universal hypothesis—one which humankind has never, in fact, transgressed. So.. why, beneath flies, are there hypotheses, why?

It would be handier to keep, on your knee or in your pocket, a little box full of midges, to get you around town; such a thing is possible, violently possible. The industrious program declined by the barouche. How vile, all the manipulating, in a case like that!

I usually took a barouche. If it slowed down I took another. I was in back of everyone, on the hanging rail, for free, but the risks were serious. I got to school on time, but nothing to be proud of!

In the tangle of these two elapsed times, I decide the horse is right, who leads you where the fly makes bold to go, because all is similar, everything converges to one point; what blindness is it that keeps men from living their truth?

A miniscule bus tried to eliminate the barouches—total flop, sabotage, the darkest of plots, nobody dared call the cops, nor lift a finger. Even though the little bus is now little taxis, the horses know that is all pointless—the little taxis will end up the same way, everything, in the end, will find its normal rhythm again until when?.. The bus and the subway, this couple is unable to grow among Barbary fig trees, and the barbarism is always the other person's.

In the street, various other chances incited my wanderings. To tell the truth, swallows brush so close against my childhood that a wild wingbeat stays with me. A swallow can perch on a telephone pole and I tell my buddy: he's mine. I throw a stone, the bird falls, not dead, stunned—a lick of saliva mouth to mouth and there you are. He flies off. Anything is possible, you just have to launch a dream of yourself in the street.

A rather soft possibility, since in the street the body has no defense against the art of the eye-blink; the body is on the lookout for the slightest trembling, but the novice, as for him he spurs himself on with eyes shut, with the convulsion of a dying man (not a civilized one). Suppose you can move one eye, two, without getting them mixed up; then the game is all in the eyelid. Opening your eye is nothing, but working it without getting lost, that's like speaking in parables, through talismans, as an open book: those who are clean and sound in body seek the body in the street, by means of an aggressive little poem, one that comes from a part of the body that needs expressing, according to whatever passing crisis, and when the veil of desire is rent between you and her, well then, speak fearlessly, you are covered, under the aforementioned terms and conditions.

Who were the workers, though, in that town? Not a spurious question if you had a nimble and lilting foot, just for that distance between shops, their bulk economy hiding its real trade. You have to find the promised paradise behind figs, dates, dried almonds.

Then the spell is improvised deep in the shop, through a release of scents, a furtive litany surrounding an ensemble of silent instruments. Inevitably, in a wealth of flashings and gleamings, I come back, as it behooves, to the frail table of the healer and inker of talismans, beside the sole candle, unlit. He says: You are divided here and there, in your body; you sleep fists against the ceiling. He says: You are haunted. He gives me a talisman, nonchalantly wafts incense at me. I then have the certainty of being protected. The road wraps me so close that the medina and its allegories echo in the labyrinth of my phrases.

If all are at home as they should be and God is out and about as He should be, you could quickly get from my house to Spiney Park, laid out—I've been told—as the Cartesian dictum has it (clear as clarity and pure as purity), and harmonious according to the metrics of military order, or of a pleasant stimulant, of the beautiful, of the True, and maybe even of a few other things. "Heh! Arabs do love to gaze upon paper roses, or plastic ones, nature has fallen through their fingers, they squat about, drunk on tea and absinth. And to hide their misery they fornicate all day. What's needed are rational gardens, geometric towns, a boom economy, you have to create paradises on earth—God is dead, long live the French settler." Such is the speech of the colonizer laying out the town like a military map.

Just one more step and you are embarked on the forbidden zone, the sacred ground of the conqueror. This was the caustic alienness I was forced to read, crossing between neighborhoods. You don't just sit Beauty on your knees, whatever the poet says (the Damned), the one who went off seeking the wild euphorbia in the heart of Arabia. Here is the Park, here a little museum of flowers and plants, whose aromas fade in the maniacal geometry. Drag your feet, rest your rear end, then look through, cross-ways, inside, and beyond. Know this: the Park is a softness that gets you ready for the tomb. Here, O reader, is the Cartesian coolness of mind moping in tree shade, and here the untouchable virgin. Forbidden, the plucking of her nipples—you must leave to the wind the scent of her four seasons.

41

I played there at times with friends, we went to watch the games of *boules* and tennis near a little bar, a piece of eternal France: a shot of sweet Martini, the ritual beret, and then some interminable game. And doesn't time destroy itself in an endlessly splitting repetition! Once again I found myself, lost in this montage of baroque images, sloping off with the troubles of the colonized child. What could we do, crushed in our bodies, if not— Lovely Occident—deflower your very nature, attack your forbidden zones and catch the little goldfish quivering in your matrix?

We know the colonial imagination: to oppose factions, compartmentalize, militarize, chop the town into ethnic zones, silt over the subdued people's culture. On discovering their uprooting, this people will wander, haggard, in the broken spaces of its history. And nothing is more atrocious than a rip in the memory. But this tearing speaks both to colonized and colonizer, since the medina always resisted with its maze.

Aïcha Kandicha, the legendary ogress whose hair gripped the rock, lives, as I knew well, in a lagoon clogged with seaweed, in a stretch of shallow warm water. By morning the eye picks out, over the lagoon, washerwomen without their veils, and from time to time the whipping scarves of strange fishermen: a silence, perhaps opaque, but the jnouns, too, have the knack of multiplying infinitely, as in the wink of an evil omen. In a fraction of a second they jump into your bedroom, toilet holes, corners of walls. In the Turkish bath they have a sweet voice, and swaying hands. As you can see, this species swallows the obtuse, the darkness, and awaits you in solitude. At the shore, I saw a *djinn* floating on sea foam. Where can you escape, as the illusion grows sharper? In the quivering stupor of the wave, I dive.

42

Later, I wrote a play that had a secondary character called Frankenstein Malabar, who strangled his victims while murmuring: "Excuse my innocence; love created me Malabar." Born from the rib of the ogress, this play has the slightly macabre taste of my childhood.

Aïcha is even my mother's name, and the women in the family embroidered the fantastic at their leisure in order to say No to the religion of the men. When they tell you "The subconscious is maternal," reply "I am the patriarch and the system is mine to rule."

Near the lagoon, the polyphony of an abandoned history may join me, I give the fortress a Portuguese name, where the birds knife into the water; my childhood might come bouncing along in my uncle's boat, my uncle often steeped in kif, a desultory fisherman and, of course, a fisher of the shallows. Happy, I suspected nothing. When I return to this fortress and linger there in the evening, I drop my hand down between wall and sea, closing myself in a soft suffering, a reverie ever more drifting and evasive.

Essaouira.

Cold, often swept by the current of the Canary Islands, the beach rises from the water, pushed by the bent horizon. A pale, mischievous glance is what you'd need, to avoid the grains of sand that attack when you turn your head, and fly up lazily, in every direction. The shore lets itself be frilled by little wood shacks, running peacefully off in a monotonous line; things fall well into place if your gaze accustoms itself, you rely on your eye and the line straightens itself, and they, the shacks, cute and doll-like—what if a gusty wind came up, one that really bit? Self-effacing waves, too, jostling each other slightly, as if to get by, they round a small island with its prison, near the port, the Portuguese empire with its emblem of huge forts, wheezy grandeur of those who thought to chain men to the rock. A city for sale, the urchins say now.

There is, in this robust urbanism, the grandiose dream of all history's pirates. There, too, the sandy wind undoing the majesty of these fortresses. I used to aim my shouts toward the sea, beyond the mounted cannons. The god of our childhood—is he dead, a hundred times dead, and hurled on the rocks?

Orson Welles shot his *Othello* there, dark, decisive, a knife. The city that played in it, recruited by force of dollars, knows by heart the theme of the assassinated queen. And thus jealousy, another queen for sale.

A shell surrounded by sand, this city sketches itself as a miniature in tender colors, and I'm holding back other vibrations: the surprise of the sun, the town curling in on itself and the scent of argan, the common element of all the Moroccan south and the soft hint of a continuous flight.

The Jewish quarter is not far, other odors, another lightly sing-song dialect that made me burst out laughing. I snatched the skullcaps of old gents, and sold them. With the money, you started over the other way. You hear that Jews will remake history against the grain, prisoners of a thousand year old difference. These are only the legends of The Venerable. Peace! Peace! Peace!

Green-eyed kid, you dump in your pants, in broad daylight, and the lordly house laughed. I was the idol of the harem, where my aunt visited her friends. I played around the water basin. Let's be clear: the sacred, in my childhood—was knowing how to separate the rituals of the body by means of water, this is useful and that is harmful by water, the West by pink paper and the meat-eating fork. They say: Child, be faithful to our tenderness, rivers will flow, this is sure, and you must flow, green-eyed child.

So many women all for nothing, a harem lodged behind my evanescence, I lost them one and all. I will turn back against you all, the Day of The Great Rending.

They, too, the little girls of my recall, pubis against pubis on the terrace, as the cats brushed against each other. The mothers yelled, I ran off into the maze, later on hashish opened the sky for me.

From my aunt's house I surveyed the street, the *haïk* veil is so much dancing drapery. My request to go down to the street then led me once again into the game of the eye-blink, women hereabouts covered their whole bodies and one glimpsed, beneath the fiery apparition, a single eye, a sole eye well above any appeal of mine. I went astray before these vague forms. Run for it...

This town doesn't live only on sand and mythology. The boats idle in the port before or after fishing. Other times, the fishermen follow the wandering sardine as far as Senegal. Starved all year, the town waits; when abundance comes, the sardine rules over all. As sometimes happens, you throw it back in the sea when there's surplus.

As a kid, when your cruel thoughts make you used to sardines and their odor, when the port falls into place in the evening silence, before fishermen ever smaller and poorer with the century—child, when you flit about barefoot in the maze of the streets, you must know your way. Know that which you don't dare, beware of the unformulated!

With one direction only, the solitary, basic way, you will brain yourself on the subtlety of combinations, you will encounter a group of cats, gathered in their moment of splendor for sardine carnage, soon rendered implicit. In this town everyone will hound your desire, who'll deny it? They will sell your tenderness—who will go into exile for you? Don't you see how they speak for you, against you? Will you grasp the atrocious truth without screaming in the wee hours? With your pal, you used to wander in this town that refuses you now, you had two mothers along with baby formula, the war wasn't over, all will recede, despite your brother in wet nurse and in every syllable.

One step into the impasse, another into a different one, I knock on the door, no one comes, I walk, a stone in my hand, I throw it, I roll it, so goes the world, by little jolts, the child that I was was breaking apart on the off-chance of finally dying, finally living, finally dying, the chance that one can live against oneself in a gap of memory.

An image comes back to me, a woman all in white, with a sharp face, who disappeared with the cock's crow. My first film was a horror movie.

I hated the romantic dramas, those songs all sounding the same and telling me that life was nothing at bottom but a simple melody, nothing but some tears at the end of the movie. I'd rather have the fist, a simple western punch, that's what got us through. At the theater, we lined up two hours before the show. The owner, a real fatty, stank of cologne and tore the tickets with a ferocious air. Well! In the intermission we snacked on dried watermelon seeds, extracting, ever so carefully, little bodies, hard and fresh, short-lived—the breasts of little girls. Already near-sighted, I had my own inner cinema, with the stinging and peeling of my eyelids. Besides, I didn't understand French. Zorro did a little dance that wasn't in the program. Though evasion was more and more my theme, I was

46

storing up suffering and death. It will be made known that Tarzan the white man, rippling and strong, steps forth triumphant in the droning of a paradise lost.

Hero of every new week, you will cross the village following the gashes of bullets. Slam the door of the saloon, it will thank you for your commanding presence; a few bandits and idle whores await you before the traffickers of death and garglers of whiskey, before the *femmes fatales* of velvety gaze. Walk face to the sun and strangle them without pact or intercession, except for those who say "Howdy!"

And So Goes Culture

Stick a school down at the end of a long, straight street, it will keep its distance, iron gate above your childhood. The grown-ups slipped in the little gate, that was their privilege, I went in that way too, when the walk led me a bit astray or the thirty-six times a year when I caused the death of some relative. Being late, you might say—what a chance for betrayal, for the child ruminating a ferocity of fingers, marbles, birds, and how to confront the little gate, kick it down or climb over it, while behind it there was the Principal, a fat pig splattered with joy, mean, and hiding at other times behind trees to catch whoever was late. A slap, open and candid, though its stars made a new silence—I hardly had time to spin around and drop, clean in the middle of rote alphabet. Deliberate order in the classrooms, lined up single file, and scholarly advancement the same; one hiccup a year, and you needed five to get through the whole school, to be declared a graduate.

My father sent me to the Franco-Islamic school in 1945. The guy who ran it was my cousin, the kif-smoker. What stood out on him were glassy eyes that crack in his voice, and above all an extreme economy of movement. I traveled, somewhat confused, in the little eternity that he inhabited. Tottering, as was his custom, with the hardened myth of seeing the Turk in everything, hardly living, working only by fits and starts, reading history as an epic cut through by the redemptive sword of the Turk, with this century's Americans and Soviets as mere epigons. A thesis as good as any for giving the world meaning. In between times, he married a cousin, dove back down into his paradise. M\y father drove him from sight, finding him nothing but a spineless hoodlum. Myopic in addition, my

49

cousin pressed the newspaper close, hardly seeing anything but highly suggestible, randomly commenting on the hazards of the day, a bit carried away by the rickshaw of his delirium.

At school, secular teaching imposed on my religion; I became trilingual, reading French without speaking it, fooling around with scraps of written Arabic, and speaking my everyday dialect. Where, in all this babble, was there any coherence and continuity?

At first I was a mediocre student, I scribbled strained and overwrought letters. What's more, I had this permanent tic of failing to keep lines straight. They will say that these letters climb, tortuous, shattering against the margin, a subtle crisis in which I measure the response to silence, to failure; mashing the alphabet that way against the swallow's dip and swerve, thus goes our culture, they talk they talk, and the sand runs on. In other respects, my road knew better, along with my foot.

I was a mediocre student for two years, but not a rebel. You get worked up, you slave, you fail in the end, your achievement in the end being that the others forgot, those who punish sleepiness, cheating, my own cheating and my huge ink blots, one's hand getting accustomed, through fear, to running wild. Like a glinting incest, this fear before the act of writing, fear of being devoured by it, at the greatest distance from yourself, and of dying as writing's conspirator at the end of an interminable monologue.

The teacher was ready to question, rarely did, never perhaps. He sat at a table to keep us alert, no more than that, he read the paper, spat, yanked our ears.

The ultimate norm, to be motivated by a loser of a teacher. And how can he demand that the chalk not squeak? A class of thirty, a kind of erosion of desks pushed aside to compress our group. We had never admired the suitability of those pictures hung at the blackboard; yet it was important to imagine their opacity, the condition of the objects, their transfigurations, and I was awakened to their very spirit in the hollow of my uprooting. Thinking how the teacher always broke off on time consoles me. The provincial schoolmarms of France really knew how to drone on—what a difference! They were our scholastic harem, and we peeled its layers, year by year, until our full maturity. We changed notebooks once a year, but punished as ever you read it face to the wall, one foot off the ground, the whole class ranged behind your head, and so turns your culture..

Since these teachers knew some fine things, since in our dreams they were *houris*, we would drop any old thing below the desk, and just like that you were down on the ground, with a side glance toward their pink thighs. A brood hen, this woman of respectable figure and diphthongs never guessed the scheme below the desks, or else she was degenerating, purposely angling so we could see. We all strove to announce our futures for her: me, bus driver, and a buddy simply to be French—a laughable career if you ever heard our class.

Plunk a French flag at your side, here is the Resident, Juin, one of The Immortals, French Academy hubbub not only of the great dictionary but also standing as a twin of the military arts. Be present on the sidewalk for this carnival, control yourself, under sole command of the schoolmarm, wave the flag, red white and blue yourself. The Marseillaise is a real feat, the first music that shows you this military marching, with a sheep in the lead. And this will be called one more hymn for your slaughter. Try to be onomatopoetic; they'll be grateful if you pull off this resemblance.

From that point to comparing my French to the language of the Koran would require a whole new scroll, which will happen the day that nothing stops me from jumping from page to page given the furious doubling of myself, and the book I write then will be one of religious thoughts. Tree of my childhood, the Koran dominated my speech while school—school was a library without The Book.

First as song, the Koran is learned by heart, and my brother, on the day of that final apprenticeship, celebrated meat and blood sacrificed to the kindness of one heart. In fact, our father read it aloud while fiddling with his prayer beads. The mothballed books of our father sometimes got this bath of fresh air, there's your arduous theology out in the sun, there's my father, one more demonstration to make in the face of the mildewed, the mystery. Next to the Koran there was the talisman and magic of women, through henna and tattooing. This is why, sign of all signs, the vagina is the end of disordered memory.

At school, there was the music of selected readings, since I knew nothing of fairy tales and cartoons. As far as can be told, we'll never know if those passages dazzled us, even though their gentleness and their characters summoned, through our own laziness, a dream world.

The museum of selected readings that the following rhetoric emerged from: our talk, in our assignments, of what was said in the books, wood crackling in the fireplace, before Rover's shrewd gaze, going out in the snow when we only with difficulty imagined what it was. Rover took cover under an Arabic name. That didn't change our guilt at all, we felt like children conceived outside of the books we read, in an anonymous imaginary world. And from one course to the next, disappearing behind the words, carefully erasing any suspicious traces. Each of us plays cop to his own words, thus your culture turns against you. But Richepin and Daudet! And many more, with an air both persistent and general: a sort of vacant lot. And Tartarin was no cowboy, let's be clear.

Now, to move on, let's divide the class into two factions, the one with some knowledge and the one that killed flies. I was somewhere between the two, if I'm not mistaken, if this memory seems alien to me, if I have the slightest control over my mirages, that is, the gallop of synonyms, bizarre, extraordinary, fantastic, abracadabric, and sshh! when the teacher looked at his watch the voice of the dunce rang out, from the back of the room, "Time passes, monuments crumble; what remains, what survives, is human thought."

Child, you must know that a series is progress, a verse is evocation and that everything cancels itself out, as it should, when knowledge lays its whip on you. Cross over the yawning word. Cruelty! Cruelty! In the vacant lot of French culture we belted out songs, bellies hanging forth, we scratched them raw, the song's flame went out, perhaps only melodramas played on a bell, and myself now a dog, my ears perked, muzzle weaving, and, through this slide into the void, I meet myself in the suspicious gaze of my double.

The same with the quartering of the seasons. In October reading passages relating to summer, as the leaves went yellow; Christmas showed up with the decomposed corpse of autumn on its back, and bing! Spring was already there! Then events cascaded, they hurried us through exams and on to vacation. My childhood, my true childhood, I'll never be able to tell its tale.

Such a melody as this, spitting back the essence of the selected readings, exactly as they were, while, like a broken arrow, the spirit of a child gets colonized. One's heart played, rather, with talismans. Of course, Morocco, in these readings, in the guise of a joyous folklore: white tunics, bright scarlet Turkish slippers, blood-red watermelons, and what could you say? The call to prayer a recording only, astride a somnolent people that only woke up to moisten its fingertips and sketch out a genuflection or two. Prayer—that was talking to the void. Amazed by this image of ourselves, we chuckled, a bit ashamed the way you are at a really prurient movie, chewing your gum to make the latent reactions hurry by.

Because history was this charging knight, disappearing in the space of a tiny engraving. Through my mother I already knew the epic of Sidna Ali. As a de-ramified heir, how could I ever swap a child's nakedness for the howling of a myth? My paternal grandfather, at the end of the last century, was seized by mad evasion. They never knew why. Do you ask a snake why he molts? He abandoned his family, got to Mecca (it's a long story how) on foot, on camelback, and in a boat that sank. He was saved, no doubt, by the inexorable shrewdness of anecdote. After a stay of one or two years in Mecca, he was back again with his family in Fez. Then, for still more mysterious reasons, he took up his adventure throughout Morocco, working stucco and marble. The end of this story finds him in the countryside, shows him dying peacefully, surrounded by children. You must add to that that we used to respect our elders as gods, our comic book to the rhythm of prayer beads.

For my mother living is a way of remembering; our family tree, in its blossoming, held the pulverization of history at a distance. This history began with the Prophet and ended in paradise or hell—I had my place somewhere or other at a predestined point since, as a child, I was covered in any case; kids who die land right away in heaven.

At school we rediscovered chaos. Turn a page and a dynasty falls—a king's head! Dynasties crowded each other, tribes champed at the bit in the dust and, from time to time, there appeared the whimsical head of a charismatic who, having wrought miracles as a grocer, raised a horde of locusts and, against all resistance, crossed a country that had seen countless devastations. Moved by this commotion, the colonial West decided to intervene for everyone's good. Hallelujah colonization! Hallelujah merry olde history!

Let's leave books for a moment and return to the city. At that age we used to stage rock fights at night, one neighborhood against another. Huddled in a corner, I slipped behind a veil of hesitancy, a thin thin child and the tribe's voyeur. When running took us to the sacred leader's place, a kilometer from town, we entered boldly, with little thought of the spirits that haunted the cemetery all around us. In the *marabout*, we dug out gems, stole small change, by this frenzy summing up our betrayal of all that was sacred. As a bonus, grass so light and thick, out beyond the tombs.

Child, the glorious day is here, go, once a year, to the tribe's rural fair. Play your gaze in the dust, furtively float through the crowd at the edge of the stony beach next to the fair. That's where the slaughtering happens; walk among the gutted carcasses, seal yourself in your insouciance, even though rutting dogs cling to each other in front of you. Such rut is an annual period of charity for

55

all comers. Perhaps you tremble, for fear of castration. Throw stones at them and pass by, as the carnival invites you in. Others have certainly aimed the vitriol dagger of your tribe, Delacroix on winged horses waving a magic wand for the West. Later, this will be a faded image of your wandering. Now, child, turn neither right nor left but go into the tent. Night falls and next to you is a young girl from the countryside. Rise, child, and bestow on her your rosary of awkward caresses and touch those hands patterned in henna. The fleas can swarm away on the mat, don't bother counting their attacks, be sluggish to the point of cruelty. The cock's crow will not sever your desire. Open your eyes and bedevil yourself. The fact is, child, this night is for a people that divides itself.

Go by the grilled corn or the rolled nougat, go by the kaleidoscope, but stop when you get to the story teller. Carried away by his tale, the teller imitates the whistling of the sword and holds his arm out while whirling around. Duck your head like the rest. It is a thrumming moment, and here, and here again, with fire spit forth, and now boiling water, your legs tremble together—Ayee! Ayee! The story teller says: the cock wants to fly up to the seventh level, and it's not that he lacks wings, but that this paradise doesn't want any part of him. Because, you know, life—it is parables that help it pass.

Before leaving this carnival, recall your peasant uncle, employed since WWII at the side of those who rule over you. He has traveled, without enlightenment, the Occident, has been indifferent to the savage discrepancy. He too adlibs now, as a story teller. Listen, soberly, to the disjointed narration of his travels.

The memories he'll harvest will be like an old gramophone and faintly scratchy records, and through the zigzagging of the needle—if a needle can really reach forth—you will see the Moroccan soldiers parading in a distant land, singing:

Why, oh why, did we enlist?
For the chow and for the mess kit.

Child, go with your parents, preferably your mother, preferably on a wedding day. During the ceremony, there are women and men, this is a sign that somehow disturbs you. Sing, even disguised as a girl, they'll be grateful for your gyrations; shrug your shoulders and say, "What do these gyrations matter!" Sit beside double-robed transvestite dancers; a violin rambles happily, it has been squeaking for ages, it speaks now with a dirty tune to lead you away from the group. Dance, dance, and bare your chest. Those who claim the bride's sheet will be white are wrong. Far from it! It will be blood-stained. The men will pinch the groom all over, before this bloody sheet, until the cool of dawn. Ouwah! Ouwah!

Adolescence in Marrakesh

One severs childhood, with a considered judgment, at the intersection of an identity that devours itself and the weariness of fascination with the succeeding ages.. And how to disperse, just then, the profusion of reflections, and ravage nostalgia? Very softly, at scene's end, there is a crescendo of memories. What mask to betray yourself with, when one drunkenness is like another and knowledge frays? A separation to be designed in a shifting whole, and so I move on, head bowed.

Leaving for Marrakesh at twelve years old! In the bus, a horrible nausea, that vegetal urge ever more aggressive which was beginning, thanks to the jolting bus, to scratch at my nostrils, and ended with the last stalactites of snot and tears. You launder your brain, trying to make sense of this passing upset, ration your breath, and that's when the crisis surges up, then sinks away. Through a gluey gaze, someone's grimace or smile, a sky and its white gesture— you fall asleep.

During this sleep an absence beaded up, neither buzzing nor questioning, the very edge of a contradicting escape which hurled him, through the heart of his bewilderment—now fully himself—far from the tribe and far from the household dead, though his mother protected his travels with a talisman at his neck. A tumble through pure and ringing duration, and the weight of fragmentary somnolence. He was dazzled by sleep, body adrift and forehead nodding away.

An adolescent's separation, ripped from his double exile, two towns and two mothers, but in the coolness of the past, behind everything else, that unforgettable bathing scene—the pool and the naked women scattering among the boughs. No madness was able to destroy that fleeting lewdness vanishing into a pointless metaphor. Childhood was about to die.

And the search for knowledge in a bus wallowing in the gravel, thus did the paternal plan push on through the dust of books. It seems I learned, by some kind of wink, by sleight-of-body, to read in a dead man and to write for the survivors of my uprooting (my generation), cleaved unto a double language. I deny nothing, however, nothing, and welcome any stirrings that challenge me!

I left, a glorious scholarship holder, shaped in my handwriting by a teacher from the Pernod and anisette school. He taught us with furor, with slaps, even on Sunday. Thus we had in our pockets a language that was heedless of the century, a French decreed on scraps from the middle of a wandering sentence, on degradable paper, for it was the Koran we respected; there where it lay, it sang of itself within and without. Parable, proverb and good news rounded out the tetralogy of our culture.

The semi-arid plain that separates Marrakesh and El Jadida is like a representation of stones, and by instinct I simplify the staggering of the fig trees, which rose up absent mindedly at the slightest flutter of my eyelids. Normally the fig trees let the wind have at them by bending over, sticking to the ground. At that time, while it was still hot, they shrank, unraveled and tender in their drowsiness. The nonchalant gesture of the sun showed me the dry brook, first and retrospective taste of so many memories; from that point sparrows started up, seeking their rhythm, the ravaged memories of childhood, making of my body a transparent and voluble image. In one move the landscape tilted, red earth on all sides; sinking within a color, in the same motion, as if in a tumbling trick, an allusion to the beginnings of distress—and stopping there, never moving on.

At Marrakesh you distort the minaret of the Koutoubia with the weariness of your voyage; after the palm grove, on the threshold of an exiled sun, what I had to show at the city gates was—instead of a dagger—a suitcase crammed with underwear. When I got to the school the proctor announced: Number 108, here's your bed and your chair, the rest belongs to my iron fist.

Jamaa Lfna Square pulled away as our *barouche* outwitted the streets. The school door was open. Our trip shut down, as we reached the dining hall; I cried, stretched out at night in the orphan dormitory. Weep, my brothers, weep, pilgrims to infused knowledge!

In the school's kitchen there reigned two huge kettles. The cook, fondly blood-thirsty, hovered over them as the flame increasingly stirred them. According to daily chance and various strategies that he knew how to crack, he grabbed and served with open arms. Strange anecdotes made the rounds, about his terrible merriment. He moved whatever lay before him with just the tip of his thumb: a gong, his moustache, and the plate arrived on crusade in a land of exiles. Artisan till the end, he plunged a kitchen knife into the loveliest of the housekeepers. Hoo! And a look of joy. Yes, get the infidel locusts behind you—crush, step out in a direction all your own!

In the dining hall, a green pea, well, it's nothing, even if it's hilarious, it has its own future all laid out, it bounces up, and you might say it gets dried, mashed, and worked without the slightest scandal, and all rejoice. Two peas, they cancel each other out, no one has the heart now to laugh, to do anything; just a couple out for a walk, or the spiritual risk of waiting delicately with one foot in the air—we gobble bread and water until we're this close to idiocy, but the fatted day (Sunday, for boarding students) there were lots of peas and a crispy pie. I was happy, and used to get a little wild. A pile of peas and the anger of a

61

proctor who said, "Number 108, get out! Take your chair, your plate and your peas outside, over there!" At the table I turn, you turn, who's going to get that piece—it's mine, it's yours, it's his. My accomplice, and under the table with his foot, aimed me at the best piece. And so the table plotted, minds a-flutter, the unclenching of thousands of cells left back at the dorm, and what's there to say, I ask you? Industrious future, miserable quest for knowledge. I was unhappy.

And then the locusts, Marrakesh shifting in the clucking sound; a locust, it can lodge down under a stone, but it takes a tribe of locusts to undermine the (hard to nibble) stork, the contemplative, cynical stork, ever higher above everyone. Stretching along the Koutoubia and its labyrinth in order to seize it required a transformation of town and country, a fluttering new mentality and a leap into the void, even though hashish created the saying in town: I keep my nose in my own business, now move on! The locust has long understood: you must avoid internal war. It has chosen a passion for general suicide. The locust, therefore, swelled with desire. A marvel! Creation upon creation, the crunch, the dance of eyes and fingers, erasings, a mad writing from which I derive, as far as my body is concerned, a tightly ordered system.

Locust or some other legend, I will recount the following upside down, in a maelstrom of suffering, before the *kafta* on a spit, for, deep in the shop, smoke and sweet flesh of the camel will sing forth.

We were coming apart. Thursdays the doctor would poke at us a little without looking, sometimes hardly touching us. He kept you at a distance, put his hands on your chest—a machine the hand can do nothing with—and yanks at it.

Others were waiting, no time to even take a pulse. In his sly way, he lived calmly at the edge of his conscience. You could doze off in his arms, to test this.

On Friday, a one minute shower for each student, on the run, wham! and the water splattered everywhere, you have to catch up to it, the sea so far away.. Like homebodies we preferred to finesse the shower, no modest spitting, fidgeting, head askew under a shower head that ogles you all over.

At times, to relax, we sprinted around the circular yard, a step here, another over there, and what breathlessness! The climbing rope between our thighs, a trick well known to schoolgirls and yielding the peep shows of our dreams. We ran. The ball blazed. Tired out just in time, we went to the hall, a somber cave—ping pong, to the rhythm of a Beethoven symphony, with Wagner waiting his turn. I took charge of the phonograph needle.

Prison within oasis, the school brushes all in one shimmer—and a shimmer far from legible if you swept up a cloud in the bunched neighborhoods—the school brushes against an endless park; a piece of wall is ripped away, red everywhere and warm memories, I fell over to the other side. Palm trees marched along the garden, this enticed me into running, I felt oh I felt such nostalgia when, taking a siesta in the sun, I briefly left the proctor's whistle, the hard chair. An apricot tree at spring's end, a theft, the fruit in your mouth, the words thus unleashed— don't tell me bitter longing is preferable, thus the tree was stripped, attacked by our drowsiness, oops, whoop, one for me and one for you, a feast of one or two hours, at spring's end. I was unhappy.

A few months' misery in that prison! Afterwards you resign yourself, here or anywhere, at age twelve, you reflect that you haven't picked your preferred ground, or parents, or parables. They chose for us, all they had to do was choose for the rest, this truth so final that it will tend, in vain, toward explosion, in vain the wake-up at 7:30, in vain classes from 8:00 on, in vain lunch and recess from noon till 2:00, in vain and yes in vain, dormitory at 9:00. In the afternoon I escaped into torpor, nonchalance, indolence, purring, grating, tingling, and now, now I tell it all, I speak; even though I clung to this pace, farther off, much farther, at the very edge of my established place in life, I hurtled into waking dream.

The school was a mosaic of neighboring tribes, for example the pale, broken faces, those from the city that would sell anything (Essaouira), I knew them by heart, with a heart that was calm in this respect, but then there was the eye, the wink; the other tribe and its dry onomatopoeia, the Berbers who did without annoying enigmas, and their gamut of gestures and the goat-song sound of them; and, behind these tribes, the innumerable sons of the gangsters from the South, they came every year, not to study at all, just to be there as support for the tribe, to protect it in case of an unforeseen uprising. These bunches of newcomers helped each other out, clogging up the hallways. We came from the North, which is just an expression, because the North shifts around, you're always the north to some north and to some south as well as to other remote places, the main thing is to shift when there's a war, to stay on top of what's going on. Our group organized itself for defense and for brawling, I transmitted this sense of order, crouched within it. Cowardly? Not at all, reader. Voyeur? But the eye is mortal, I've known some to waver when faced by forms. I wasn't! Not at all!

Boarders by idiom, we distrusted the day students, the ones from Marrakesh, who weren't really brawlers, gifted instead with a sharp sexual style. The chair or any old thing became an erect penis. These disarming—shameful—allusions placed the seed of hysteria in us, and we attacked. Smack him! Hit him!

Obstinately refusing to fight, the day student's words were his trenches, words that demilitarized any tribe that was there. If you divide up a man, one part for a woman, one for a man, what is left? Our answer: the infinite precaution of shifting a chair, calling it "vagina," and only by surprise "chair"; knife will thus become desert, and by surprise knife, and a knife on a chair? The mists drifted still. The Marrakeshi toyed with the boarders in his obsession to desire everything, and we went crazy. Hit him! Hit him!

To this subtle business we preferred the hurly-burly of the nickel brothel, pulling whatever from our pockets, after a session of chewing gum. Don't spoil your women, we'll all be grateful to your flowing on by, thus the world dances. I was unhappy.

In class, a chance to accentuate my near-sightedness, if nothing else. The eye started, just like that, at the end of the piece of chalk. It has been said that the blackboard outlined itself, in an instant, with a bundle of graphs, the deep reviving of my litany. Distinctly now, I open one parenthesis within another, to separate myself, body and past, into a book translatable by little cries. And I cite that math teacher, a frightful fellow—red hair, a crab's face and what else I don't know!

He swept the room with stiff gestures and aimed first one then a second question at us, knowing neither had a real answer, which was palpable to us. You flunk before you settle in, as the schoolboy's language has it. And we didn't have the rejoinders to neutralize him. More and more stimulated, he made the whole experience a boxing ring, running everywhere, writing and erasing, ending up leaving the blackboard, racked by a savage howl. Yes! Hurray! Little in the way of resistance from us. As for my pathetic, somewhat wretched air, it garnered only disgust: zero for effort, and on top of that his obstinate refusal to correct my work. Other teachers came, throughout the day, to clean up after him. Some gentle and persuasive, others as lazy as you might want. To tell the truth, often they would let us go with some disjointed discussion, jokes, or anecdotes from daily life—with a weary satisfaction. One well-read Algerian, caught up in easy paradoxes, splashed about in fly-specked argumentation that showed his love of contradiction. He was about right for us, this baby-faced dialectician, so easy-going that it led to doubts: we got together afterwards, galled by an absurd scrap of learning.

Here's your geography teacher, squat, hissing and pointing his ruler. With a wave of his wand mountains sprang up, inhabited by strange sing-song words. Mountains now questioned, submitted to what, exactly? Like a station master without his cap, planted in the center of the universe, he watched over the extremely complex course of rivers and streams, measuring, verifying; always, deep in this, there was a litany of minor barbarism. We pressed the mountains, out of curiosity, to challenge the atrocious silence of the universe. We were present, as well, at the splendid show of Niagara Falls. Yes, beyond the plains, the high places, beyond the desert where even death lost its memory—the true domain of geography. This science, a dusty unshelving, nudged us—towards true chaos, an un-tattooed space. At its limit, in the distance, the sense of the world became confused with the mathematical swoop of a swallow.

Strange land: geography gutted itself with the rusty metal of citation, while I went on dreaming of unbalancing

66

every fixed site with just one aroma. I retired to a corner, ingested the lesson, and recited it before the good professor, zigzagging through the periods and commas. Back at my seat, detachment was born again. Because this same teacher was a good raconteur of Greek mythology. It was a marvel to me, though the number of gods startled me, and their familiar and calculating ways; a marvel— and what good was the dusty history of cultures to me, if I could not dwell in the splendor of their subconscious?

When the heat lengthened our collective wandering Marrakesh unfolded itself, more enigmatic than ever. What woman with studied hand would have given us, along with the henna's spark, the enigma of this labyrinth? The Marrakeshi pulled back, a people who moved little, but in those moments disappearing in the blink of an eye. On the outside, vague whisperings, an extreme fragility of hands, and somewhere the emergence of palpitations— muffled, secret, and scattered. Sometimes the brutal hollow of the sun, then the town was reborn, dappled with lights and perfumes. Various furtive shopkeepers knew well the fugue of it all—this way opens unto kif. We have readied for you, green-eyed adolescent, behind the basin of water, respectable ladies, each caressing her pubis— you have only to chew some hashish. The heat! The heat!
Beyond all that, set a rendezvous in a corner of the fortress, hold yourself upright in the palm tree's caress, hold on, innate material for a turbid city!

Green-eyed adolescent, free on Sundays, you stroll Jamaa Lfna Square, around and around. Before you, that man swallowing boiling water, dribbling and then smashing his brazier. Don't blink, he will pretend to rip open his stomach, he will dance. Elsewhere, the snake turns over, disappearing into the void. The Saharan snake charmer gives it a calm stroke. Rise! Know your true direction in the face of all these precipitations. Expel the hippies and their pathetic goods. Stroll on, be indolent and proud. Take hashish once as an experiment, a second time with humility. You'll gather your classmates, you'll expatiate, with fire and stars, on a single poem. Preferably Baudelaire, oh green-eyed adolescent!

If you still want to, have another hit, at your aunt's in your parallel town. A girl will come to seduce you on the canopy bed, dim your gaze half way, so you can just see the ceiling and the rest of what happens. She will come in on tip-toe, will lay upon your chest the faint touch of small hard breasts, let yourself drift! Open your eyes, the room will be green, not paradise, but a licit inscription out there, in desire. What desire? Often it is the whorehouse you hesitate to enter—then you plunge, with longing eyes.

Truthfully, that's where they will choose for you—deep in an adjacent street—a woman, perhaps without make-up, perhaps captured in a triple garment. Signal her to come on up, even if your sign is sarcastic. Unclothe your penis, the boarding department now moving to a side-show, adding little warmth to your blood. This girl, shier than you, will make you dream of what, exactly? Amaze yourself! Ever dramatic, as you pluck away her light robes fold them in half at her languid waist. She'll make tea for you, stir the tea, green-eyed adolescent! You will cross through her, towards what—with nothing to hold against your tenderness, nothing to hold against your explicit puberty!

Tomorrow, you'll awake and you'll be fifteen and sad and disfigured.

The Body and Words

I dreamed, the other night, that my body was made of words.

You are always the adolescent of someone's dim memory. The happiness of writing is what saved me. I owed my salvation to friendship with books, and to that teenager with wild hair who cast an ironic eye on all he saw. An inseparable duo, a friendship that was always renewed. He drew, while I wrote poems; he sang, I improvised bits of songs. He devoured comic books, made the teachers' authority seem nutty, teachers we sequestered in our intrigues, by collecting their tics and slips of the tongue. We ruled over literature. To write, to write well, became our terrorist technique, our secret bond. And we passed through years, borne by an inexorable fascination. I became a public writer; on Sundays the boarding students needed me to dictate love letters for their girlfriends. To stir my inspiration they brought me photos. Surrounded by my dictionaries I was exalted and multiplied through these epistolary passions. Thus I was in charge, till noon, of the world's emotions.

Poetry did the rest. The Bedouin was what I first loved, burned into allegory, that of the pre-Islamic bards and above all Imrou Al Qaïs and his tender incantation. He lost his beloved somewhere in the desert, passes time caressing his horse, and disappears in a flight of rhyme. I put away from me the shrill times, my expulsion into the street or the brothel, I played at disappearing into words, I gnawed at verse, stored lines of poetry in a little yellowed notebook that I reread before sleep. From day to day, from image to image, a thousand lives passed each other, the whole thing thronged, I came away with a wild and happy brain.

Another exercise: shuffling books all around, making a jigsaw puzzle of them, a delicate coming and going that was cool to the touch. I read novels, wrote still others, and, in bed, these bewitched demons carried me toward such sweet fatigue that I fell forward into dream.

As soon as a novel ended, an elegy drifted toward me, wavering, beyond its great speed and its irrevocable tension of flights among the lines; even a lousy one sang like the parody of a voyage. I was, randomly, wellspring, flower, butterfly. Reading brought me back to life, to death. The scent of a word would throw me. I trembled. What frenzied work, swallowing the dictionary of rhymes, and that other one of synonyms! And on top of that, I took the book from the author and made it the speech of my own mirror. By establishing my tyranny, I cleared such a book of its rot, and saved—for the author's good and mine—a few phrases that I immortalized in a notebook of quotes, taken in one casual stroke from all the most famous writers. The professors said nothing; I seemed to have an irreversible power. I especially liked the strangest words, which opened the heart of some far country to me. More than a stumbling discovery, it was a silent and glacial hand-to-hand combat; after the instant of joy, I checked them off with a savage color, to suggest to me always their definitive relationships, and I said them over and over with my eyes closed. Faced with the explosion of meanings, I avoided trying to understand—it would have been the end of my soul. Understanding was sweet death; I contented myself with their least clear and most treacherous glimmer. As with those dozers in the cave, words were born at my command, escorted my steps, and—as reflections—doubled my godly efforts.

In the yard, in the dining hall, I smiled absent-mindedly at my classmates. No one knew the power of my doubling; I lived, untouchable, in the chanted solitude of my being.

Pulling back the covers of my bed, hiding the candle, far from the proctor's eye, I regained in a fury the book I had lugged around all day—with one or two extra books always in my pockets. In our communal life I was neutral, disciplined, neither more nor less unhappy than the next, with a mad, unexpected laugh, out of nowhere; they had a pretty good idea of my drifting. The proctor's marching orders started out but, when they got to me, dissolved into bubbles, bubbles, bubbles. I forgot my chair, my body cleared itself of all muscle, and crazed among words.

My rhythm: dreaming while the others worked, reading when they slept, running away, always running away, watching the signs of the outside world through a hole. In the evenings when I was Julien Sorel, like every adolescent you find in literature, I swapped my boredom for vanity, I floated, immortal, from the end of all ends. Dead or alive, I thought about going off, through the night, to create a new religion. They sent us off to the dining hall. I didn't leave Sorel for a second, and how was one to swallow doughy slops like these with languorous ease? They got used to my trips, and they relegated me to a manor house. When I was back among the others I veiled myself with a coarse gaiety, smearing the air with gestures wide and grandiose.

At the beginning of this century, a sick poet left his native land. He coughed with a dry cough, and stretched out to sleep on a mat. Did he allude to some sign of complicity? Once given breath, his poetry faded into incantation. He pronounced the first word, and suddenly there was humanity. At first a weeping willow, Gibran little by little made himself a prophet. He declared it himself: I am the son of Zarathustra. Soon I mixed the two up. One died young, he knew this was to be, I too knew I was going to die young. A dream soon to lose its bloom, which exiles itself now in this adolescence, I will

71

have died at least once in words. The other one, right to the end, studied an inextinguishable madness. At fifteen I created, from afar, my image as exiled prophet. But where? My incantation was somehow dull, my writing a poor excuse for parchment.

In the evening, after dinner, I used to walk, head bent among colonnades, my right hand strangely crooked. I was imitating the depths of solitary people. Someone would pass me and I would give a strange look out of innocence. If they interrupted me I slipped quickly away. I was someone else, a whimsical quantity of time, alive with fervor. Having this kind of alibi, I parked society off in a corner, I made myself solitude's vassal. Living, day and night, off borrowed dreams was the absent image of an unreal body, a body riddled with the plain raving of a ringing desire—never named and easily gotten around.

The most tormented of my comrades and I, we were always looking for a shock; history was there in front of us, and we flipped it around: if the Arabs had beaten Charles The Hammer and conquered Europe? Seduced by the West, we removed ourselves from the distinction and tried to erase its memory. Must one choose between dream and history?

At that age, I chose solitude, and literary brothers. My preferred gods were marginal poets, the suicides, exiles, crazy, tubercular or dead young, the very ones I knew to be forever lost in pure suffering.

In class the classics marched on by, in the role of official gods. We swallowed them bit by bit: every year one tragedy and one comedy, as a way of keeping their burbling sounds in balance. With some luck you learned to hammer out *alexandrins*, that frayed meter that led us toward an unexpected dance, thus does culture dribble on.. To dazzle us the French professor would close the shutters and shout while running around the room. This was his totalitarian approach to getting us out of ourselves, offering us a culture that was frank, robust and inevitable. During his class ritual replaced culture and the sound of iron replaced the interior song that had carried me along. We reopened the shutters, a fleeting moment when the body knew no limits; the sun entered again and he announced: literary explication. On the best days we put on theater scenes. This somewhat pathetic theater transformed us, and we jumped about happily in a jumble of questions and answers. The teacher had an assistant who also yelled. We seized on the repercussion of his shouts to rifle the silence with our own sneaky creaks and squeals. We kept up with him until the final collapse. And at the next sound, the professor thundered. I kept still in my place, my feet actives as bees. On the arid plains of Corneille, I lugged my radar about, I shot out tightly-wound *alexandrins*, (cylinders of smoke, though), and these sucked away my breath. Here the rhyme could finally be unhooked from its knotty dryness. I imagined benumbed camel drivers with their swords stuck in the sand, awaiting morning to pick up their trek. The Cornelian characters whose tirades I frequently had to step over left me with a steely boredom. At the end of every play everyone gathered up his dead—me, I filed away the "tribe of words," and then I waited.

When I jumped a grade I attacked *Cinna* after burning through *Le Cid*. Not caring for heroes, I was on the side of the fallen gods. Most likely, what attached me through some fiber to that sonorous and quartering universe was the recalled memory of a glacial rhetoric and fearsome incantation. Corneille was one of the last armed prophets and, by means of his feudal universe, he brushed stiffly against the disheveled myths of childhood.

You couldn't mention one without debauching the other; I cite the balance that exists between Racine and Corneille.

73

Up to us to choose. We chose nothing. Everything fell, already spread, among hollowed-out identities. From acquired culture, you put together a collage. The teacher posed the following conundrum: "Suppose that Curiace kills Horace—tell what happens next."

The kid in front of me solved the problem with purely administrative style. His beginning was completely frank: "I have the honor and the regret to tell you that I have killed your son." Culture didn't interest this kid, he simply let the chair hammer its way into his ass. He wrote the way he greeted the principal, confused art with censorship and words with their arbitrariness. He called the writers by their first names; we let him get fresh air on his own, and only brought him back to show him off, when the Cornelian dryness was absolutely killing us.

A maniac for imitations, I continued the story through laborious, nicely buffed *alexandrins*. I wanted to please the teacher of French language, since through Corneille I might have entered the eternity of The Other. The West offered us her paradises. I dreamed of being a literary quote, a god among gods. For a whole week I had applied myself to bundling *alexandrins*. Savage and epic for an entire week, I finally achieved the excessive state of cosmic rhythm. Whether the plot ended in a fish-tail shape or not, I was already on a level with Corneille, from every indication, with the teacher at the center handing out the parts to earth and to heaven, and finally, down below, to the croaking amphibians.

A few times I dared, thanks to my readings, to dress up the official gods, to neutralize them by feats of imitation, first identifying with them, and then, since this closeness weighed on me somewhat, swerving sharply toward a parody that I thought de-colonized me. Docile toward my idols, I tortured the rest, adding bizarre morsels to their works, all drawn from my pullulating, tyrannical, mobile library. Hugo, who was dear to me, got off scot-free, attached to his bell-like rhymes. With Racine I took all kinds of precautions, reading him before falling asleep, even if the finishing touches on his passions threw me. For my body called out for a nostalgic song, while these characters based on suffering and death-in-love astounded me. To the sublime I preferred reedy sadness or furor, or aridity: the utterly romantic, complete with mythic arsenal, lame gods, and a mania to poetize everything. I drifted. What aggressive or orphan story could grab me away? I was waiting for time to unravel, for my real life to begin the exaltation of a new life. If adolescence is easily given to the nearby cry of conversion, in my case I think I just hoped reality would give me a rude shove. History was passing by, I was in my little hole observing myself wake up, study, eat and sleep among others—acts short-circuited by a haggard voyeurism.

I was writing, an act without desperation and one which was meant to dominate my sleepiness, my wanderings. I wrote because it was the only way to disappear from the world, to pull back from chaos, to hone myself for solitude. I believed in the fate of the dead, so why not wed myself to the cycle of my own eternity? I hesitated in my choice, not wanting to pay the price of that suffering; I wanted to be joyful when day removed my mask, with a whistling, uprooted, undeniable gaiety.

Thanks to my older brother I branched off briefly toward modern Arabic novels. From that era my first Arabic poems were born. Let's wager they belonged to the wind, or my notion of it, since I didn't sign them.

Now let's allude to our adolescent poems, let's mix them up a bit, as one should, and without regard to their now-faded emotion. After rondeaux and sonnets, following a seasonal order, I sharpened some sincere free verse— verses of parting, either wheezy or chiming. For example, in committing to paper the evening's romance, I allowed myself to dream freely, to tell the world to keep silent, so that my tuning in was really felt. Well! All of nature came to my aid, completely vulnerable to the power of my graffiti. My little metempsychosis burgeoned so well that I turned away disgusted from my all-powerful nature. In the vagueness of autumn and after sleeping too much, dreaming too much, I departed drunk from the end of a sonnet to a romance of some kind. "Dear heart!" I cried out during these two days, "Friend, my sweet friend..."

And if rhyme broke and streaked away from me, in seconds, I would wait peacefully for other miracles to stammer at the tip of my half-broken pen. Now there was inspiration! The word, esthetically, included a graphic that was the emotional résumé of my fascination with the blank page. Who would have dared prevent me from making "cold" and "code" rhyme, while trembling at my own audacity—who?

Disgusted with this innocence, I began to parody others' poetry, and mine too, the choppy, succinct hiccups of my own work. While imitating Prévert, I would finish my poem with his kind of pirouette: the young man has grasped everything a young man can grasp when he really understands nothing about girls.

I had to come up with someone to dedicate all this passion to; carried away by poetry, I fell in love. She was called Sweet Dove, I was Sad-and-lonely. She wrote for "Literary Thursday" in *Maroc-Presse* and I did too. This dedication lasted two years. Love, so I thought, would do the rest. I desired her through the written word, she responded with unintelligible sighs.

While waiting to see more clearly, I took long walks, and, in prelude to my fantasies: haunting women that I waited for at the turnings of streets. Nothing came, except their image in my rhymes, and I fiddled with that and avoided all scandal.

Green-eyed adolescent, you speak my soul, and then, in the brothel, you descend into craterous vaginas. Your adolescence was a dream. Propped against a whore, you stake out a thigh and absently follow the smoke of a still-burning cigarette. You come back to her, you glide over the sidewalk afraid of being recognized, and you find her once more, already emptied, eyes wide open.

Now, as sweet Dove shows up for the first time run, newspaper in your hand, this will be your password. She'll arrive light of foot, floating in, and her dress will call your hand forth, truly dancing. Relax, loosen your tongue, for flitting between the two of you will come sober phrases, fine and sensitive. You take a step, she goes even beyond that, she throws a hand back. You stop yourself, she sits, making a little dent in the seat—and what a miserable posture for you this unpacking of everything, your life, all your waiting for her and your little travails! She smiles, her chest gets a bit adventurous, the farce is complete. Of course, you think you'll get all of her, next summer. The truth is, she'll leave you there, in the garden, with a newspaper in your hand.

You'll travel once more to meet here. She'll arrive, there'll be run-of-the-mill disenchantment, she'll freeze with sunken mouth, shaping it like a delta, evincing solitude. Fight back your tears and take off! Speak: goodbye, epistolary art forms, goodbye nubile poetry! If you must keep trying, get a new girl, court this fat myopic, she'll hug you with teeth chattering. You'll reap only fatigue, though her dress will be over her head. She's looking for a husband, and you, you desire a woman. This will make a strange selling point when dealing with others like her, through all kinds of crazy contortions. Settle your cute little heart in your defunct poetry, there remains only the supreme body to conquer, for you, for others. And then, green-eyed adolescent, you have a head full of thoughts—believe me, history is stalking you, you will be.

Through Uncoupled Moves

The country's Independence was at hand. My evasive youth suddenly awoke to the call for action. I was coming out of a meandering childhood, though a protected one. A guaranteed future—I saw it in culture. No mistake: writing is, in this sense, an extended adolescence. I saw myself as a writer without taking stock of the needed suffering and vertigo. Writing is a way of surviving memories, floating through time, like a bold, confused leaf.

At the boarding school I latched on to the slightest flight; falling quickly back to earth, I looked for the sign of some shock, some binding reality that had perhaps clouded my awakened dreams.

Sitting down again, I withdrew into myself, in a reverse spiral, and—what exactly?—I waited for the wind to pick up. Negligence, you might suggest: I wore socks that didn't match, dressed any old way, grew used to those neutral clothes you sink into never to reappear again. The hairbrush fell from my hand; forgotten somewhere, it could barely be troubled to fix a fleeting grimace, one hair that wobbled astray from fatigue, a bit of music set to the vast intermittent invasion. I liked the inertia of my body. From tribal memory I have not inherited the warrior's strength, rather the wisdom of indolence, and I could long follow the wafting of a perfume. Choosing the moment of desire to inaugurate each time a whole world, that was my right.

It's true that there were exploits in the imaginary. Seized by an object, I let myself slide, and by passing my hand over them, opened hermetic closets. Nothing stopped me, and if the doors wanted to close I forced space open, the spaces that were assuredly articulated by some demoniac insistence that came from my magic fingers. Someone would give me an order, I'd forget it along the way, then pick it up again by its end and carry the fragile thing some distance. Inclined towards others, I braced myself for sparks—they crackled around me morning and night.

Between disillusioned reality and myself an extraordinary sneer persisted. By uncoupled gestures, and in the middle of a conversation, I froze a sentence, word upon word, as soon as the fog became really thick. Exiled from myself, I split myself into cheating creations of gaps, minor madness, and hum-drum. Knowing nothing, saying nothing, all the while articulating humiliation.

And here the warm epoch of history and action. Protected by its God, my society shook up the old litanies, white anger, in effect, little by little—well beyond a childhood nourished by a rotting, heart-breaking history of the Second World War. An uncle told me about the bloody butchering at Casablanca; huddled in his house, he listened to the machine guns in the night air. In the morning, he got up very early to distribute the daily *Al Alam*, which was half blank pages—everyone could guess why. With my older brother there were imaginary assassinations everywhere, and we amused ourselves filling empty time that way. And in my real dreaming, I truly sat with Marx at the October Revolution. At school, political action, any way you looked at it, was tortuous. In an episodic way a few tracts fell into our hands, and we interpreted them in groups. There was no internal organization, only the sabotage of the Other's security: to rattle a colonialist teacher, we used to write DIEN-BEN-PHU on the board. Since the class was shot at that point, he would insult us, take the opportunity to call us vandals, Visigoths, barbarians, and many other rather forced names that sang with their own terror.

A passivism then came together, spurred on by myth and rumor. My mother contemplated the face of Mohammed V (the exiled king), on the moon. Continuing these efforts, she ended up seeing the whole royal family there, and I didn't hold her explications against her, for my mother could tell me so much before each of these flights. An explosion of legends, so long dormant! This dreamlike power protected our evasions into history. As for the rest, freedom sprang forth through the palpitation of the body, and, the next week, by exchanges of good luck.

At El Jadida I evolved into a highly mobile demonstrator, switching neighborhoods with no set plan; the labyrinth of streets offered the key to anyone who knew how to zigzag between aggression and our underground forces. To escape the paratroopers we disappeared into wells and cisterns. From the terraces, our look-out post watched the sky ripping open. Naked, direct confrontation was rare.

A paratrooper kicked in the door, noticed us, my brothers and me. Hands up, shoved along by the machine gun. Arrival in some shed, interrogation. I was slow in explaining to a cop why I was unshaven, and he slapped me, screaming, "Look at the floor when I'm talking to you!" We stayed there for hours on our knees. For lack of any information, they let us go, while marching some others off to a vacant lot. An incident that wasn't really shattering, that taught me, later, to act with precautionary humility. Combat requiring, as it did, subduing any useless pride, I picked up the habit of semi-clandestine acts. One time I vanished into the countryside where I urged some relatives to at least saw down telegraph poles. Elsewhere in the country there burned, if not fire, at least the power of myth. On Fridays, we protested with prayer and shop closings. An old man responded to an inspector, asking who had given the order to close the store: that it was a holy requirement. A natural way to fox the Devil! From every quarter strange voices rose. Rain, it was said, was

81

going to vanish, the sun would surely drown in its own fever. We foresaw the end of the world. Surely, the Day of Great Violence!

When I think how, at similar moments, whole societies had felt the dizziness of death right up to the end, and how they had been forever swallowed in the song of their own throat-slitting, I know that man can swing back and forth between life and death, in exalted indifference. I also know the very point of vengeance for anyone who came back from that strange land.

Passivism reorganized our anger. Invincible, we resistance fighters dynamited, grenaded, assassinated and then disappeared into the depths of a well. The women preserved the saving power of talismans. Since with one hand they pushed evil away, and with the other they intensified the clenching of desire. The labyrinth of streets once more came under the women's protection.

Beyond the chaos of history, we fed ourselves on the hidden power of merely enduring; for once, tenderness was divided, without jealousy, between mothers and the streets. Action rediscovered a distant memory.

My own action was relative and unorganized. Several kilometers from the town they were executing some resistors whose gestures and words reached us dusty and ashen. What! Death was becoming strange and quite lovely. We commented on a condemned man's spitting in the face of the assassins, this man already on the edge of the grave while the machine gun shattered him with accelerated rage. We hovered around the base, then returned to town along the rocky ways and the sand— there's your cry of colonial history, sewn onto my body.

Maybe the rootless nature of my action derived from my constantly moving between two towns, the one of childhood and the one of my studies. You got initiated into the terrorist act, a skirmish improvised over a poster, in a garden, against a police officer. Destroying the self-assured gaze of The Other, then disappearing; inscribing, in this way, with choppy streaks rather than with chitchat. We followed on a cop's rounds, in order to project on him the foreshadow of his retreat or his death. The trick was to multiply the cracks in this space through flexible parables.

I let myself be taken once in a while: thus, one atrocious night in the hands of racist doctors, after a routine tonsillectomy. When I saw the operating table I had vomited a good portion of my blood. Stretched out, I listened to their conversation about our ingratitude and barbarism. They had control of my life or my death; but my heart was excellent, I came through it. This long nightmare, which I underwent with eyes open, tortured me all night. I lay awake, my hand hovering. To pass the time, I imagined myself fleeing the hospital and killing myself somewhere on a cliff. A whole collection of nightmares marched by: my ever-roaming childhood, a movie of humiliation and vengeance. Doubtless I died then, a winged image, a flash of light through the window. Then what?

In the morning, a white nun came and rubbed my head, offered me ice to put on my tongue. My mother was there; I was not allowed to talk. When, back home, I fashioned gestures for my illiterate mother, she brought me a cat instead of a stool, any old thing instead of any other. This game of irrelevance was refreshing. I laughed with my eyes only, happy. I rise with the crow, I remain alone, I descend with everyone else, I rise with the swallow and the owl—and swoop!

At school, where I had always thought of myself as a clandestine passer-by, we began to detect who was an informant. When I felt particularly generous and futurist I wrote bloody poems about these rats. A poetry that circulated freely, since symbolism covered up the

83

operation. News flew to us from Marrakesh—always discordant, already mythic. In his prime, the pasha of the town propped his victims in a hole and then bricked them in, as rumor had it—butterflies whirled to their death. Later, he foundered in drugs: paradise, the harem, numberless offspring. While he lingered among these delights, the town wondered if he really existed. This phantom glided, underground and omnipresent. Resistors plotted his capture, plotted the blood on his *djellaba* and in his eyes—eyes so glassy, so burned out that snakes were thought to coil their glowing coils in them. I was a witness to this whimsical reality. I showed my identity card to the ever-present cops, in my fearful and dislocated way, never forgetting the barbed wire scratching across my gaze. As the town was changing over to a new syntax, this deep but narrow old man, the pasha, was hurtling toward his end. The phantom was doubled, thanks to a king taken from the kif world. Fragility, the spell of appearances, lugubriousness, all brought together.

What an end, to bear your old age this way, lynched by derision and faithless history!

They came to our school, the pasha and his double, one cool morning. They assembled us all to watch the show; we were hoping for an assassination. Watch dogs up on the terraces. The sun rolled along, there was a kind of ripply music, no surprise fantasia. As the phantom's beauty was only beguiling at night, we were left with nothing but a pallid misunderstanding.

It all marched on.

At the town's mosque a resistance fighter screwed up everyone's scenario, fashioned the first image of the death of this pair. The accursed king, still dumbstruck, demanded a calm and official tomb, with a kif pipe as a souvenir. But at Rabat, instead, they put him on a gilded throne and turned him over to the crowd. Our attempt failed again, the act was cut short and our resistor was already sprawling, riddled with bullets, tattooed forever.

Rebellions awoke on the tops of mountains, uprooted from their natural soil. A peasant with an old rifle, all alone, making his fight into universal war. The unforgettable epic of our adolescence! Dazzled, I rediscovered strength from another century.

Right till the end Marrakesh lived, even though renewed, within its limits. When the pasha finally knelt before Mohammed V it was already the end of a long colonial ride. Autumn brought back the exiled king and other princes of the resistance whose every act and word we had learned to spell. When he came down the gangplank the people wept.

What was happening to our town? With a firm step and relaxed gait I strolled, assaulting my childhood, haunted for the longest time by tangled hypotheses. Withdrawn into himself, or packing his bags, The Other cloistered himself during the festival, the joyous murder of Father, Son and Holy Ghost. Do I have to say it again! We now had a five star aim: little settling of accounts, we reinvented ourselves in the encroachment of some of our original truths. Independence was the irresistible happiness of an identity dreamt until delirium.

Listen to the song of youth, giving rhythm to the parades. On the platform a little girl, her hair in flowered braids, was reading a speech, red and tremulous, then, to applause, she went back to her mother's warmth. Someone praised the crowd to the skies while blessing them all. What an image!

In the street everyone sported some fetish or nationalist fancy. You changed constantly from cause to effect, with a snap of the fingers, you passed on, chest thrust forward. Brandy Boy, a popular rascal, acted out little comedies—

often failures—with a handkerchief, went off again, bottle in hand. His sustenance required a narrow footprint. If his head touched the pavement in a morning's excess, he began to meddle, slowly and from afar, with the dimensions of an excuse, of its grimace and its crossing through. He came and went, gesture and mist, finding a brief nest, withdrawn from his misinterpretations. A lowly and rosy Sinbad, he gave himself rein in various downhill collapses, a real point-blank drunk; it was the street's vague prison that sent him back to us in an about-face, with his sublime gaze, the stage-player of all he surveyed. An inexorable drunkenness, from bar to bar, an ending of life never fully drained. He knew better than anyone how to expel with just one word the weight of mortals.

We set up a make-shift theater in our neighborhood, and the peasants from the area often came. My older brother wrote an impressive play, in one sitting, for two characters, the former Morocco and the new Morocco; I played the former, he played the new, the whole thing being thoroughly derisory, and with the monologues all delivered—as an aside between you and me, my brother— it didn't exactly make waves.

Another item on the program: a man sleeping. There was an alarm clock that was supposed to go off, you waited for it, the alarm clock slept on as well. Nervous, the audience began to fidget. Now the sleeper was snoring, I urged him to get up, get up, he rolled toward me, swore at me, fell peacefully back asleep. I let him go on, and waited. Finally he rose! At the very moment that he was about to comply, the alarm clock exploded in sound: he was left, standing, hands in the air. For a few seconds he then acted out the sketch of two fleas loose in the room. He suddenly scratched his armpits, everyone laughed, I whispered out a little song, and in the fog of my comings and goings on stage, I listened to all aspects of the play. Then other characters filed by, armed with sticks and stomping in place, long live Independence!

There appeared, one day, an obscure individual who proclaimed himself a new prophet—white robes, completely self-assured. He spoke very little, hopped on our stage as if it were the rightful place of his dignity. With one gesture he rid the place of all our props, then meditated at length, rigid and majestic. He stirred up the crowd. Go on, he said, open your hearts and your ears, you'll hear the most beautiful of beautiful stories, I am a cobbler, but I have learned the secret word. He spoke, left very slowly, and was followed off-stage by an enchanting and interminable spectacle.

To respect the growing demand of our public, we set up in the town's big theater. On the program: poetic plays in classical Arabic. At the end of the show, the audience was still sitting, having understood nothing of this literary language. One of the actors yelled out that they could leave, it was over. This failure ended up giving us a rationale; we took refuge in tradition, the only way to seduce. We took up the magician's wand, the perfumes of the Prophet. The audience laughed readily. Our youth, the abused companion of our youth, our youth of the most distant memories now served to spell out the people's every fraternal word. In this collective singing, new to me, I felt happy, guardian of a new freshness. Beyond its disillusionments, that era still holds my greatest and slightest palpitations. Like a childhood that has never gone astray, history has the scent of an euphorbia—unclear, and at that time invading me.

Unveiled adolescence—girls, I mean—before our eyes. For the first time we had formed a group with some girls: afternoons at the beach or in town, a series of rotating evenings; you were on your own to concoct the whispered approaches to desire, with—for starters—tea, Coke, cookies. We gave ourselves the name Blue Moon. We did two generations worth of dancing, tangos and rock and roll. Slow dancing was a problem, if your caress went beyond the furtive brush. One girl swore to her mother she wouldn't dance the slow numbers, at least that's what she said she'd said. The girls lined up, us facing us. We would jump up, make a turn, with hands clammy and sex well-behaved; when the latter started its own dance we would suddenly lead the girl in an unforeseen pirouette. We debauched ourselves elsewhere, with uneven performances and between very different thighs. Within this group, what we had was more freshness in its unconsummated state, the prenatal recollection of a slight embarrassment. History, which uncloistered these very girls, offered us little loves that passed by in complete openness. When the girls left, we would reconnect with two intoxications, booze and whores: "Melancholy waltz and languorous dizziness," said the poet I liked at the time.

In those days we would have liked to experience the fusion of tenderness and desire. What fearful theater was bewitching the nest of our long wait? To open the encoded vagina you had to bind yourself to someone, while I always felt myself confident and free. Every age has its failed or blotted-out desires; I had the promise of the future. The fact is, I felt little connection to these pale evenings.

Already, that year led me to a taste for philosophy. I had started up again at school. All the festivities didn't stop me from working furiously; with my high school certificate in my pocket, what vocation lay ahead?

Marrakesh got rid of Jamaa Lfna Square with a puritan edict—the brothels were erased from our geography. The Pasha, under the weight of events, gave in. They smeared

88

everything with a triumphant moralism, trying to clean away a long servitude with one swipe. Tradition seemed, for a moment, repressed.

I discovered philosophy with a liberal and deeply Christian professor who had been through the concentration camps. His friendliness touched us; a few years later, when I started my first course at the University, he was there, hanging around with students, as unpretentious as ever. At Marrakesh there were only four of us students, and before class started we nibbled a few warm doughnuts together. We were one war late in catching on to Sartre. A short time before, I had had one of his works in my hands; it had quickly seduced me, even if my lack of grounding in philosophy kept me from completely getting it. My understanding was drawn to the rustling of the words, to the outrageous metaphor, to the sinusoid curve of it all.

I was next to soak up the signs of my own anxiety in Sartre's novels, even though, in comparison, my anxiety was on the frivolous side. The Sartrian world was anti-Christian and anti-bourgeois, while mine was magical and epic, overlaid with masks, and my mind and body colonized to boot. From all evidence, the way our beings were divided up was different, and my oblique connivance with Sartre only reaped—in that era and from his particular universe—a few sonorous samples. You might as well say I chose little slices of him, but slices that had more knowledge and more bite than my own revolt. Born at the beginning of a war that was not ours, I had grown up during another combat to get free of which the West would pay dearly. So there was no passionate identification with Sartre, a minor prophet with fluttering cigarette who was conjured up in some extrapolation of my own anguish.

Between the two of us, rather, it was a play of shadows—let's say, a thankful greeting, murky but decisive. Through him I participated in the crumbling security of the West. This Occident that was beginning to doubt itself and was living the luxurious phantasm of its death. With each war, the West re-enacted God's death, and at the same time surfaced again looking blinded before this splitting off. And if, at times, the triumphant West sang of its own Nietzschean loss, what about me and my own culture?

I recognized in their culture the random piece-work of learning, the repression, the change of scene; I grasped the flaw of all this in my intimate self. And because I was tied to this seduction, I lost myself in the weft of desire. Loving The Other is really speaking the lost places of your memory, and my insurrection which, initially, was only history imposed on me, continues on as an accepted resemblance—because the Occident is a part of me, and I can only deny it to the extent that I struggle against all the occidents and orients that either oppress or disillusion me.

Sartre gave us a reason to move on to our own inner drive. If man is this shadowy history, then I felt myself to be both future and novel flower, moving feverishly, and randomly. Farewell, Occident of my adolescence! Another history was beginning.

The philosophy they taught in school, picked up in fits and starts, failed to unclench our stomachs. I sought culture in a poetic banquet, unending and made of my own foreignness, borne away by the matched flights of some rhyme or other.

Here is an image brought back from the recent past: me, floating. In that last year at Marrakesh, when I was a nonchalant proctor, climbing over walls at night to go to the movies, I was drawn to the whims of the moment. I saw a lot of two Algerian teachers, great fans of both kif and *L'Internationale*, and we mixed our pleasure with cynical meditations on war, revolution and death. At the end of every month we rented a coach and headed to the casino; a small luxury that didn't leave us with a scar, only the multi-colored shimmering of money. We courted French women and Jews, so long forbidden, we reinvented speech; I stared at the illusory barmaid, the vehicle of a thousand repeated images, slaves in a gaudy castle. Somewhat sobered up by all this, we hopped in another coach, with the same indolence. Indeed, there has always been life in lazy ritual.

I've never known how to act in Casablanca, despite my natural politeness. What had I become, the following year, in that town? I thumb through a book about the town's recent past, from early in the century. I pick out a photo showing an empty stretch by the sea. A few traders squat there, the neighboring tribes often washed up there, since there was no place further to go. A city that was an echo, and made of the dust itself if you believe some of the survivors, a small port you could budge with your little finger, and a population that looked the other way. Now, an earthquake, down there, makes the skyscrapers jiggle with violent but harmless jolts, just to bring on a little fear—this city can tremble, no one denies it. By hiccup or by shudder, the city's organizing principle is propagation with no convincing reason, there's no map, not even a military one, to figure out which street you're on; you have to count on your fingers, logic requires this rule as a start. You'll understand, I hope, the reasons for my rudeness, or for any other phenomenon. You end up in this city any way you can, any way you want, the main thing is to get used to the noise and to stay at all times deep in your head. Otherwise, fleeing is the only thing.

At that time in collective life they made do with a town crier; the crier related whatever entered his head, rumor dwelled in his head, he kept it there for everyone, and the populace slept peacefully. As he was the final prophet, handsomely paid at that, the crier took advantage of his power, barked out orders that became briefer and briefer. No longer able to hold back the haunting in his mind, he became so fantastically thin that he blew away with the last attack of locusts. No more town crier, a town beginning to worry, no more water carrier either, his spring had dried up and he was found one day dragging in the gutter, a sad business.

The whole city, without crier or water carrier, dreamed of lost paradises; in the dream the water suddenly went salty, and the cry turned to horror. To give themselves courage they went out in the street, howled above the sound of machine guns, pulled up paving stones—what good were those stones, for what? Long live Independence!

There were still a few water tanks for resistance fighters, you took shelter there, if nothing better appeared, to escape the police. No ladders, by the way—just zip, up and in, in the blink of an eye. The wells were the most awkward, they still are, as they only hold two or three people standing up. Those on the outside thought they were wearing them down. Elsewhere, still others—the great ones, those who always rise to the top—had the idea of short circuiting rumor by means of an infernal little device, the siren. This is how the city grew, an industrial miracle even though there seemed to be no logic behind it, nor the necessary or let's just say immanent conditions, the city grew, standing off against the world. If a car took a chance and tried to completely by-pass the city, all bets were off for its golden years. In these exceptional moments, you just drove straight ahead, up to the last wall you could see, then came back.

It happens, as it does to many, that I visit relatives in Casablanca; they grow as fast as the city, there's no way of knowing who or what you're dealing with, but one day you'll know. A better idea: let yourself be guided by a principle of rotation. The wind's direction is from the sea, the people head in the opposite direction, though the city's clock, all alone, is completely indifferent. Thus it will be said that I will come again among you, on the Day of Great Violence.

I cut straight to the doughnut seller, wobbling on his perch; he flattened one out for me while I waited, and childhood flooded back; the morning creaking of my gaze.

On leaving the *medina* everything came together in a faded image of the West, uprooted and now in a neo-Moorish style. How to recall this city when everything flowed together in one explosion? From afar, the ghettos ring the strange, moving fortress of the city; trembling, I cite this humanity and its beaten retreat. Everything shifted in its geometry, a city with opening drawers.

I went to the cornice to blend into the swarming joy: piercing and alert boys; girls went by in bikinis and high heels. I gave a thought to my lazy, disjointed, floating desires. Here's something you can do, there are other tricks: wake up at eleven, doughnuts and spiced tea, take the bus to the sea, cast a poetic glance at the sand. Naturally, I escaped into interior monologue. Nobody was waiting for me, there or anywhere, I imagined ethereal rendezvous, my way of surviving; I saw the ocean swell, come nearer to me, I glided toward the water, staring at the sky. Sometimes I fell asleep, slapped about by dreams of rage.

93

At school I found my cubicle again, along with a chain gang who were getting ready to apply to the top schools. I prepped for Propaedeutic Letters, passing my time reading, or listening to the radio, in the school's lounge. The initiation of new kids took place without my help, enforced by the rod. They made the victim write on the blackboard with his nose, a piece of chalk wedged in one nostril; or sometimes they stacked about thirty kids in a shower stall. Atrocious adolescence that wants to emulate, so feebly, the military.

By the dappled light of these skirmishes, I wandered with a book, thinking only of the end of the year. I went mute when baited: irrelevant to the system, a simple voyeur, I therefore learned to hold my peace, to side-step any challenge; I became untouchable. After a few months I made some friends, we hung out together with few repercussions. Downtown: movies, fleeting flirts with schoolgirls in blouses, one of whom—spicy tasting—showed me her thighs (while keeping her eyes closed); we rolled around, over and under, for a while, then I returned to the low point of my trajectory, the bare hall of the school. I collapsed in a corner. And here's dinner again, and its airy stories. Everyone revealed his little adventures. We had wine as a sedative—there was little to be proud of!

A more intense life for me was the classroom. For the first time, I found myself in a group that was mostly girls and French. Seduction became my all-consuming passion. I worked in order to dazzle, and I spoke a language not found in any book—since, as I yelled out, by proxy, "The flesh is sad and I've read all the books."

The literature professor figured out my game. He helped me. While he was explaining Segalen and insisting on the death of cultures, I knew he was arming me. He showed up every morning with his body already shattered, bitter but at the same time nonchalant. He hardly ever rose from his chair, walked around clearly talking to himself. I liked this lonely fakir, lost in a group of spoiled, colonial kids. He sensed some unease, and, to avoid total self-destruction, he incited us to talk. I once gave a poetry explanation which ended, for my public, with the curious cry:

"Oh you who hear my words, go back to your homes."

There you might recognize a note of the poet Laforgue, who colored my pale decolonization. Because these girls that I desired so deeply were caressing me from afar. They used to say that I was not like the other Moroccans. They accepted me because I was similar, annihilating in advance my whole childhood, my whole culture. Faced with such a complex pleasure I grew a mustache and sprouted a multi-colored silk tie. And this personage gave himself a certain debauched air. I was teaching others how to write their own language. They applauded, little more. I was looking for an irreversible victory, but there was only a smile, and surprise. A heedless passion that ended up convincing me of my solitude. The field lay open only for poetry, my criminal lands where my wound carved itself. I took on the difficult writers, Mallarmé, Valéry, not to mention the closer sweetness of Eluard. The game was to open myself this way to a veiled existence, and through words I became my own god, out beyond Casablanca, on the whole a detestable city which had stolen my speech.

Paris, Left Bank

The colonial that I was, read his magic table in the drifting of time, the gaudy display of Independence appeared covered over with its own cracking, one which I would have to read without losing my soul in it. And the colonial West remained a disguise to cross through.

I was leaving for Paris with no story behind me but that of a touchy student, searching for a different image of others, and of myself. In this light, I remember my vacation in the separation between two spaces, trembling slightly, sitting in a plane at night; a dream which, since my earliest childhood, had grown old in the telling. This flight was to go meet the Occident in a voyage of identity and savage difference.

Must it all come out? Before setting out for Paris no promise to my mother to come back in one piece: just to leave forever, inebriate myself or lose the ancestral fire of my tribe. She accepted my nomadic temptations, and she wept, for she knew I was becoming a bit of a parody.

I was introduced to Paris by a friend a little bit older, who had lived for a long time in my childhood quarter. Settling in at Morocco House (at the University)—a memorable link from my house to my exiled adolescence. He watched over my education and my introduction to sin. He was serious like a father and mischievous like an uncle, it was like a family scene. A few other students from my town had joined us. This group lasted for some time.

After checking out my room, this friend advised me to buy some tea and a hot plate, and, of course, spice bread and biscotti—"That always has a nice effect," as he said. He then showed me how you manipulate the light, for different romantic situations, but I didn't have a red lamp. Since this seemed to be a scenario without a plot, I asked a neighbor, who was a painter, to smear some paint on my dull lamp—and I had all I need for seductions. As we walked around the city, we reflected on other cultures. Space was selected, divided up, and all I had to do was examine the future in my own way. At restaurants the itinerary was streamlined—eat it and beat it. In the cafeteria, each of us regained some friendship or some desire. Since my arrival, I had inherited my little group, and we often got together after all our work.

A few days later he suggested we go chasing girls. Everything went as planned: pretty name, foreign, a long and symmetrical face, stumbling a bit over her words; we foresaw the rest and waited. She went on talking, smiling, with a somewhat absent air, easily accepted our offer of dinner and dance. When she rose, her build suddenly stretched out infinitely. Flattened by this woman who gave us a stiff neck, we took the Metro, already discouraged about the whole thing. At the dance we palmed her off on someone bigger.

A first experience that initiated me into the nuts and bolts of cruising for girls: how to catch the gesture or carelessness of the other, how to draw it out with your speech, how to talk, always talking to the point of disgust. I hated this humiliation, the empty hours, this mute and blind desire, this fakery stifled at the slightest sign of danger; I was, after all, a mediocre adventurer, shy and without a saint's persistence. My friend didn't believe in the other approach: letting them come to you, circling round them closer and closer and fascinating them with a sudden start or clouded look. In this broken down distance Paris opened up, always changing its thickness; I strolled from café to café—a suspended loneliness.

In the middle of the night, someone knocked at my door. The *chérif*, the Moroccan nobleman, was standing there, offering me a fairly rotten apple. He always came from afar, always called me brother. He went to sleep in a corner. After running through an unimaginable fortune, and burning all his identities—fallen prince, Polish, Iranian, scholar—he ended up broke, as always; tireless, he took up his life again. To earn a little money, he started a political party, with himself as the only member. Despising a neighbor, whom he accused of belonging to the Muslim Brotherhood, he hatched "operation stolen message." To prove there was a plot he put a message on the door, pretended to sleep, and spent the evening reading. At midnight a crinkling of paper; too tired, he had fallen asleep. The next day, the message had apparently flown into thin air. With some friends the vow was taken to exterminate this secret association.

When things were going well, he chased after fat women, he offered them stuffed pockets and handkerchiefs; in these amorous moments he wouldn't greet you, looked crosswise at us, and if someone came up to him he took off in the other direction. A tender heart, nonetheless. When it rained in Paris he used his umbrella to ferry women from one sidewalk to the other, for hours. That's how I met him, between two red lights. Farewell, *chérif*, you are truly on the road now! Paris tore you apart, but the day you come back to your brotherly childhood you may find rest among the earliest ghosts!

Here are two images from my first month in Paris. I was suffering from a sorrow without emblem, but my patience was tough, I looked like the lost soul who is half-present in his shadows, passing by and disappearing in the glare of a street corner. A strange betrayal of my schoolboy notebooks: I believed the universe took a similar path.

Recreating any landscape in the middle of this gloomy crowd, dragging your feet and sitting down in *flagrante delicto*. In the Metro what they were reading was read for me, they spoke of far off lives, it was all the same to me.

Three years of prep for a rather shallow sociology certificate. A rather lazy student, I was always looking for other pleasures—which the city refused me. At first, sociology was a bit like military service, perhaps a search for identity as well, some paternal memory or a decorated return to my country. Go figure! Seduced by the West, I longed for my own deciphering, I floated, learned from books, always separated from myself, the vacillating drill of waking up in the morning to the nothingness that loomed.

At the Sorbonne a little fellow with a tortured voice offered ferocious sociology: going down, all year long, "the series of landings into the depths, back and forth between macro and micro." He ground his teeth, persecuted false prophets—living or dead—burst out with a particularly Slavic (I'm told) laugh, in any case a laugh of terrible suffering. So my introduction to sociology was lacerating. The Gurvitch episode was at that time unknown to me; I attended, in a meditative way, his last shining, as he was carried away towards pure raving. Nostalgic for the October Revolution, he told us with great emotion about the inexhaustible excitement, the mad liberty and the sense of time itself dancing in one place.

Once at the head of the class, he grunted left and right in a furor that hardly sweetened our servitude. We hardly dared approach him, you had to either speak like him and his books or disappear—I chose a prudent silence. This god had Aron as a rival; we hesitated to form real
meaning in our exams, mixing everything together and hoping for general confusion.

What is left of all this bric-a-brac? The evils of decline and exile, the debris of a sociology without spiritual leader, but still I owe to Gurvitch my obstinate reading of Marx. Now fall, grandfather!

Of course we preferred his assistants, who were a more literary group. Their class was a relaxation period, given over to seduction, to goofing around with the girls, to giving lots of examples, with as many double entendres as possible, our little barbarities of poetic language and obscene knowledge. You'll note without surprise that our generation produced Régis DeBray and an obscure writer or two, others took off to the bush to make their ethnographic concoctions. How could we have been anything more in this brief shiver of history?

But I had some very warm feelings at the Sorbonne, my friend Jacques and my friend Pierre, both orphans, exiled like me. With Pierre, I rediscovered the fresh air of the countryside. Preferring painting to his studies, he was happy with the finest meal there is, some bread, gruyere, and red wine. He talked about his childhood and his fields. A cloudy nostalgia drew us together in this crazy city.

More secretive, Jacques had a chimerical beauty that really got to the young girls. We had a common passion for esoteric ethnography and jazz. Our idea of fun was gathering amazing facts, and for a whole year we studied "modes of humor" in extinct cultures.

You had to practically break down the door to get into his tiny maid's room, on the Saint Louis Island, in the Seine; we sat by the record player and listened, while speculating about other societies. Through the little attic window, your gaze swooped down over Paris and its airy, vague stretches. And that teenager whom I loved like an alter ego showed an incisive kind of meditation, he knew how to talk about his own detachment in worlds of enigma, solitude and myth.

Before my arrival, my image of Paris was purely literary, falsely Sartrian but ten years late. Well heck! I'd been dreaming of jazz and quivering thighs.

As a prelude to such images: the cellar cafés of Saint-Germain! Through my dance partner's hand, I reshaped the beating of a pulse; our doubled steps intertwined in a fleeing movement, I messed up the rhythm at times, doubtless moved by my somewhat perverse confusion. A few words out of my dry mouth, then finding a seat again, surrounded by smoke and hollow time. Above all I loved the most intense or sophisticated notes, like the voice of Billie Holliday, detached from any empty wailings, she who loved life as a child and who knew what a downfall was, also John Coltrane's fire, an anguish that still spurs on my writing. Music is, inarguably, the fascination that loosens my fingers. My body listens—I'm a writer!

For a while I made little entries into the Paris literary scene, poetic circles where a few survivors of heteroclite movements acted out their tragedy. The melody?—flaccid, you'd have to say. The food—expensive; it was hard to discover where charity might flow. These pale poets, brutally gripped by sublime outbursts, gave a whiff of the Comédie Française, but in a winded kind of way, with a sighing air of apologizing for being among us. The show was always there between mouthfuls, your hand stopped, you admired the grimacing mouth and the metaphorical gesture, the background music did the rest, quickly wedged between words. We ate well, joked around, the silences were unbearable, throaty shouts were ripped forth along with mellifluous first names. In the end, you really didn't know who you were most dealing with, the barkeep or the customer with her bare chest: and if the poet, a miserable type forgotten somewhere in the furniture,

102

showed up to slip his words in, he was happy to deserve a meal even if it were dog food. The druggy, she was a fork-chinned aristocrat who sat swallowing her words and dragging on the general babble, breathed deep the hardest poetry, of a sort that gave her a macabre complexion.. throw that on the bill as well...

What was happening? In Paris there are as many cities as suggestions (thank God!), as many cities as groups of foreigners, as many neighborhoods as there are other neighborhoods; in my exalted moments I had the intense desire to pass through everywhere leaving behind a wooden leg or platinum blond eyebrows.

The Latin Quarter was my dump, my sand castle, where I buried my bookish adolescence, while the master singers slept, eyes sunken, in the Seine. In each oasis there is a lair for mirage; I believed (was I really thinking?) in the halo of famous cafés. They would point out the spirit of the establishment, the writer would pass by, supposedly absent-minded, then sit down to his beer shandy. The password: let him work, but I didn't think that was possible outside of intimate solitude. Thus I discovered writers and great pretenders who did their sighing in public—and the shame of writing! For them changing cafés became a major event, a real revolution, complex plots to arrange the chairs, always meeting at the back of the room. There were always a few girls, of a palpable sort, who were an undercurrent and who never figured out the secrets of the gods. Life went on singing, muted. As a weakened ethnographer of the Occident, I observed it all while playing along, you had to get near the gods of books, those men, dead and cold, I had been served in the weekly press in Morocco, I kept up with their dilatory moments among mortals, and as soon as the season threw down a handful of dead leaves they lined these cadavers up, they ranked them by merit and not forgetting the

103

diaspora of the anxious and the bizarre. By spring, they had used everything up, they set about striking new sparks between critics, and went off on vacation, having exhausted the carnage without spilling either blood or money. And they made little lists of the books you had to take, off towards the sun. They came back well-tanned: to seize again on some idea in the air, dig up some name or other, force some theory to flower. Paris, culture, and the plotting mind!

I liked my rum-and-milk, my gaze blurred by the girls bouncing by. And? Robbe-Grillet and Godard? The talks burbled along, who-I-like and who-do-you-like—and what expertise! Let's just say I didn't know what to think at all, Robbe-Grillet is a guy obsessed with walls, a methodical maniac and, how should I say? a smallish system of smallish tics. Godard? a middle-schooler on his weekend, who was shrewd enough to snapshot the random sign of his times, he daubed out a few moth wingbeats in the blink of an eye. The Paris I haunted recognized its phantasms in this supreme Narcissus, surely it was all fake; as I had no prejudice against what was fake and because the delicious delirium of cultures is a joyous eyeful, I went to see his films to discuss them afterwards. After all, I was there to make time pass, to unbind my tongue, not to run away.

To pick something out of the air, I preferred Vian. He loved jazz, wrote really funny books, savaged our consciences at a time when war was churning out cadavers. He paid with suffering, disappeared like a wanderer destined to be found again along the journey. It was this freshness of violence that linked me to his memory—he knew how to live, write and die all at the same time, a happy gift.

All of that amounted to little, a minor flirting between culture and a lie. Inexorably, Paris appeared as inexhaustible speech in which I would have to decipher

104

my own enigma, I changed neighborhoods, wondered over a strange street, came back again and again to the Latin Quarter, nostalgic and spent. With Moroccan friends I sometimes arranged a night of multiplied minor pleasures, and somber bars where abandoned saints presided, sucking on their cigarettes and running their gaze over you, I had an empty wallet and a Muslim body, hadn't killed anyone, no longer sorry to be alive—this vision faded in the night, no dream of dying love-struck by a barmaid, however *fatale* she might be, only of following the shifting smoke.

My taste, never belied, for these sophisticated images; I floated in an out-of-body languor, the flowers were artificial, why let myself be crazed by their dark seduction? We laughed hard, the alcohol was no madness, rather we simply endured a dry deprivation of memories. Now I know, if friendship doesn't derive from a memory it improvises itself in conspiracy with the present, as if time, in this double movement, was evasion from an image never lived, never deduced.

We used to end up at the Halles loading-docks, over burning hot soup. The morning slipped slowly in, we wandered a bit before sleeping, first whisperings of the sun among men. Everything spoke very simply to me.

I was just arriving in Paris along with the Algerian war, already breaking with the West of my childhood. On the university campus we put up a few Algerians, the police kept their eye on us. They grabbed me on the steps of the Metro as I was keeping a girl company. Midnight. In slippers and without any official papers. Fear of winding up in the morning Seine, unrecognized, unseen. They rounded me up with five other guys, I waited for what came next in a pent up fury, I naively tried out a little

105

blackmail—it just made them laugh. They dropped me on a bench in a police station; sliding onto the floor, I passed the whole night, harassed by a toilet's constant flushing, the ravings of a drunk, and the lone cop who wanted to talk. They let me go in the morning, they had nothing on me. They sent me back to my studies, I took the Metro, slippers gaping, dreaming of taking to the hills, my way of ending this gap in the paragraph.

I knew the drill for dodging the racist challenge: in a foreign land, did I really have the right to look the other person's disgust in the face? When his hatred had no purchase it could cause him to decay; I suffered from being the object of hate, and I hoped to be able to forget the insult—but the gambit was tempting. Just once, before the street-person who baldly asked me, in front of an alert crowd, "You take the French for a bunch of jerks?"

"Yes, sir," I replied while idly counting the stars. Already my anger had faded; content, I left, unburdened of my soul's little cry.

At Morocco House we trafficked in the future and petty politics, torn by ideological coups and beautiful quotations. I leaned towards Marx, and still do; a split militant, I chose action when it called out to me, but disappeared when it became pathetic psychodrama. Being a fighter in the class struggle at Morocco House became a sort of literary myth, groups formed according to natural affinities, devoured each other, only to disperse when back in the mother country. One interminable revolving of adolescence hidden from its desire. Ideology can be a treacherous rose who abandons you on a street corner. We got ourselves up in the colors of the season, we let words have their way, life was simple, and all you had to do was let yourself go along.

The Algerian war tore into this, here and there. A writer without a résumé, I passionately discussed national culture, national identity or none, revolution and Islam, and since each French group had its token Arab, you had to listen to endless confessions. The token Arab said, "I am a hyphen between Orient and Occident, Christianity and Islam, Africa and Asia," and reams of similar stuff. Poor Arab, where did you end up, reduced to a series of hyphens! I saw some who went begging for some image of their identity in newspapers and magazines, flocking to the slightest deletion of due recognition. "Go ahead," said the Pharisee, "insult yourselves this way in our language, we'll give you credit for using it so well." The writers I have described in a lousy book of mine—my first love child with the West—wrote like grade school teachers and, on top of everything else, you had to grant them a meager and passing glory in view of the great cause of the oppressed. Girded in his beard, Sénac, in his actions, imitated the fakir, calling everyone "brother." Others tortured their pens in this cause: folklore stories, as a minimum to hide in, and at the other extreme the hallucinations of the split person who was no longer sure of the sex of his parents.

We got mired in war and death. In the street, I ventured little signs of concern, as I did with that man who followed me ferociously, without any reason I could think of, and who might have been dreaming of my murder, but tirelessly the war always became word again. The person who felt split made his little confession, and everyone deemed it a liberating cry. Worse than an unexpected knife: abduction of the mind. And so the colonized intellectual struggled, in the abbreviation of his most vital roots. I was grateful to Kateb—our best writer—for arousing in me a mythic encircling, a ring against which all history frays. Nedjma, marvelous incandescence!

107

With this wandering poet, I relearned my childhood path and its enigma, the distracting memories when war pressed down on me. There is speech that will not come forth except conjured, I linked myself to Nedjma, I walked a little tipsy, with far off gaze, since Kateb's song, contrapuntally perfect, guided me between chaos barely held back and blank adventure.

In the ebb and flow of the war I felt somewhat free to circulate: movies, theater, art galleries. At the Cinémathèque, I was discovering a family-like world where boys and girls jostled each other, mentally irritating each other in a languid way (but, you know what I really mean...). This hall scooped up survivors from everywhere. You got your money's worth, the minor pleasures of sinning in Technicolor images. We argued fiercely about shots that were cut, and, just as in the edited excerpts I read as a child, we enjoyed zigzagging between the commas. There were important weeks where everything palpitated with Lang or Chaplin, you devoured the images, braced by a sandwich, because you dragged with you a sad stomach, a sagging body and a sweater inside-out. We flirted between films, spent weeks that way, got the movies and characters mixed up, all to the eternal rhythm of the reel, such a slender line to the real.

I came in order to get a little melancholy and, when it let out, I trembled in front of my beer, thinking I'd drained the world. We were silent, the reel dreamed on for us, we made reservations, felt ourselves warm, generous and ritual. Paris neutralizes solitude, gives to each the exact change for his exile, bleaches *ennui*, and makes the most solid resistance waver. Like most people, I made do with the scattering of signs. Feeling yourself truly contemporary, gliding into that dazed duration in which men name themselves center of the world.

At the bookstores and stalls my hand ruffled the pages, I read shorter and shorter fragments, everything mixed together, I came back to my place tired, having accomplished my secret duty. In moments of ecstasy I ended up reading only the footnotes, hoping to see myself, some day, rising beyond this incredible intrigue of dead characters. What despair, to annihilate yourself so meagerly! I had no taste for erudition, though I had bitter nostalgia for it, I lived by double proxy.

We wanted to sample everything, if only on tip-toes. And why not painting? I had come to painting by way of Chagall, the landscape of my childhood, seen once again in that universe where magic cocks blended with motley souls. Cherkaoui was there to initiate me into Klee. An adorer of mauve, as a memory of figs, this Moroccan painter (he died young) taught me well about color, in a tumult of shades and parables. Elsewhere in my life, I would fake buying art books that were out of stock, they arrived in packages, and it was all so simple, so tempting to throw the bills in the trash. To put a fine point on my melancholy: I take a magazine, check off the art galleries by order of urgency, then run off to my destiny. Before a painting, I feel so alone that my first movement is flight, while others take their leisure gazing over it. One painting may last me a week, and my optical rhythm, if I can believe my failing eyes, vibrates with less and less force, in proportion to colors that turn out to be frightening, unbearable. What's more, art galleries have the chill of cemeteries, and the West well knows this taste of the beyond, minted in exchange for the suffering of painters. At the door are fine women, a bit stout for vestal virgins, who hand you the catalog with a well-faded smile.

If I am not quits with my past, either recent or distant, I let myself into a theater that was once the scene of a strange ceremony. A character was singing of the eternal power of the finger, everyone was shouting, exchanging masks, yelling until the spit flowed. Exasperated, the audience was filing out, not at all in good shape. Lavelli had achieved his goal: to terrorize. That was the end of ordinary theater, I was happy I had seen it, though the overflowing of magic was unsettling. I remain faithful to the Brechtian principle of distantiation.

Later, in the wings, I went up to that young man, so haunted by the rites of violence. Just like that he put on a little play of my own, a fable meant to be cybernetic, about the death of art. A series of whimsical characters, Mademoiselle Cocorico (the *femme fatale*), Frankenstein (pardon my innocence, he said, while strangling his victims), a poet (in my image) " with an unhealthy voice and a huge pencil in his hand; a philosopher in a white shirt with a child's neck, a painter (the image of my friend) with two degrees of abstraction and obscene drawings on his chest, Monsieur X, an officer late for a war, with apparently no hat, spectators must not get too worked up about details, finally a slender wino, rather a wino whose slimness was rather juvenile, his tuxedo worn with much importance and consonant with his mustache and nondescript hat" (*sic*).

The play began with a universal declaration and ended with an equally universal death; between these two events they lynched the wino (who had become mute), accusing him of "stumbling, muttering, grunting, horn-honking, screaming, swallowing, chewing, biting, spitting, spitting everywhere, on the ground, on the ceiling, on the plates, on bald heads, on the republic, on purity" (*sic*). Disgusting character! In this play, then, I had said it all and I was rather exalted.

110

The rehearsals and the show went by in the most complete derision. Lavelli was supposed to pick young actors to promote their careers, the show was reserved for those who opened the way to young talent. The actors marched by stammering over this text, impossible to read at first sight. A young and faded girl, accompanied by her little dog, acted while venting strident cries, and, to confound us, sinking into the most dreadful silence. Sickened, Lavelli got rid of the young creature and her dog. In the end we succeeded in rounding up some tenacious novices. At Lavelli's side I learned the way you "recreate" an actor, make him transparent for any imaginings. He worked the voices like a musical score and broke down any resistance; little by little the actor emerged beyond the play and its characters. Here I discovered an unexpected doubling, and my earlier passion came back much stronger. With my life questioned this way, I silently plotted my future transcendence.

Lavelli likes a somewhat crazy eroticism. When the beautiful actress playing the main role took off her bra an old lady next to me yelled, "Ah! I knew they were coming out!" Frankenstein didn't break his stilts; the play, in the end, seemed to be a success. As a reward, they offered the beautiful actress a chance to star in porno movies. So much trouble, all to end up masquerading in the Trafficking of White Women! I had thus created a new theater where the author, the director and the characters no longer have a purpose. An admirable technique—for destroying art and recreating life!

She was waiting for the Metro, standing between two suitcases. I came up to her, bidding her to let me dream of whatever place she was going to, no matter where it was. Vacation was approaching. She had a fine, sensitive heart,

111

a dancing air, blue eyes where my own depths went astray. In the middle of this winter dream that took her hair this way and that a sad wisdom enveloped us, bending to our very gesture. I saw her as a cross between fleeing time and the surprises of innocence. She lived and slept in silence, I was waiting to read pleasure somewhere on her heart. In the Metro I recited the tragedy of the dikes and of Van Gogh, whatever thin knowledge I had of her country. She winked, kindly took in my ravings, thanked me on tip-toe, that was how she referred to her village, doubtless snowbound. Through the window I tossed her my address, some fruit, some magazines. Touched by this first encounter between the rails, I waved my handkerchief. The train pulled out, I headed back on my subterranean way. Goodbye, dreaming girl of the North—that I loved as a backwards nostalgia!

This was the period when I held on to my penis instead of my pens. Go figure how to work all that out! I imagined everything in advance. When the girls showed up I was already somehow other, and distant; suddenly I would come to again, I would fall even lower than before, clinging to the bed, my legs excessive and trembling. Opening a window, taking the cold blast, guilty of having to love always in suffering—I who only wanted the rubbing of faint pleasures.

I connected through my little black book, a checkerboard of complex rendezvous, spur of the moment rendezvous between two Metro stops, rendezvous with two different people set for the same time (distraction or compulsiveness?), assignations for hot chocolate, which I hated, I went from one place to the other leaving my date to pace, I had no watch, but I did have a nicely unbalanced memory.

In my room, sometimes a blues song to dazzle, my pipe at a rakish angle. I simulated a hanging on her stripped body, music and caresses crumbling before my eyes, I didn't always get away with this routine. I would rescue myself with cold water, or a date to munch on. What a desert it is, on the very edge of hysteria, to touch one of these cockteasers! The truth is, I felt fallen, to the point of nausea, distanced from my most furtive mirrors. In my room, I waited for night to come. Inevitable disaggregation of the body! I was a solitary man, without aspiring to the glowing consciousness of that state—really, I was barely the smoke from those detached caresses.

Nowhere more than in the Metro, I felt the slightly macabre presence of bodies, to be specific: that visceral hyphening between me and the unknown woman, she pushing forty, frizzy hair, she who poured out the jumbled anecdote of her day, she of the inexhaustible leg-spread, for she wanted to wait up for the dawn in my hands. I left her a bit later, with an ice cold penis. Entwine me with that flabby body, but in the coiling of its own birth!

Was she anything but reminiscence, that monstrous woman in black leather, who spun my dash up the spiral stairs? I hardly recognized the reflection of loss in these creatures,, I guessed at their gestures based on my own, I went beyond myself when I reached toward them, strange desire to surpass myself through and beyond others and me. The tattooed feeling of my body continued, crazed through with violent spasms; I'd get home tired from doing it all over again. My member and a thousand masks ripped off, therein lay a cold truth where blond hair, a gaze and fleeting curves all lodged. I went on living in a state of real expulsion.

I had forgotten the girl from Holland. She came back, first through the phone, exotic, sandy speech, claiming she'd been losing blood. Hoo! Virginity! Little stains of both blood and pleasure, we really went at it, and who's the worse? She shadowed me, waited for me when I wasn't coming, I was going crazy knowing I was at odds with myself, everywhere I went. Still, she wished me well, and gave all she could, that is, unto my full will, my own void. Pathetic will, since I had no idea what to do with her. Helpless, I dragged her from café to café, she smiled the whole time in complete innocence. An interminable trek across Paris. The idea of running away, with no plan, catching a bird's flight or an abrupt look, I dreamed of being on the other side of each of these breakaways. This was how I evaded myself, from one glance to another, in the game of mirrors, like the viewer before a certain type of Chinese fresco: as he becomes one of its characters he can involve or detach himself depending on the grace of the story teller, as if the real and the dream were all one scene, and that scene an illusion.

In order to deserve that fine and slender body, I had made myself get used to the exegesis of silence. We lived without a spoken past; when I probed for her buried memory, all I got was the blank page of a girl's diary, and what was left was tenderness, dancing and hazy, dancing at the edge of what, exactly?

We took the train in opposite directions, an ethereal correspondence floated between us for a time, everything then got muddled, and, like a stork faithful to its daily route, I now hover over the hidden zones of that plumage.

After a whole summer in Morocco, I came back to Paris, expecting other loves. I was already less wild, I let people come at me in their own way without seizing on their misunderstandings. Somewhat detached and vaguely disillusioned, I ordered up a bunch of new faces—it was simpler and less tiring. The interchangeability of little girls, one creation after another, and, in this way, I played god. I organized others according to my chance moments and their own plots; at the center of life I could go on caring about books and taking up the play of culture; every new experiment of the mind found a ready accomplice in me. Alas! I guzzled everything without discernment. Because my body was as the future, I linked myself to the blind adventure of the century.

I saw a new girl for the first time in this droning state of the soul. A passionate she-wolf, she came to me with trembling body, whirling in Wagnerian overtures, Wagner was her god. Surrounded by records, she drummed her fingers, wild, limbs splayed, tragic to the last spasm. I shivered in a corner, the lone spectator of this end of the world, an end so distant in this sordid room that I was draining into the coolness of a glacial love. I looked her in the face: the long features of an abandoned child, a somewhat languorous mouth, hair unfastened, body slightly arched, held in place by the indeterminate shadows of her fingers. She didn't really pick up objects so much as stab them, or break them, and she often stumbled right in front of me, embroiled in intrigues that remained invisible to me; interesting, with each new day, but this aggressive unawareness of space made me nervous.

Because of her, I hung out in Wagner clubs that brought together people of every sex and age. Eventually I could make out a few old ladies, attracted by something church-like. I suffocated shamefully as the record creaked away, no hope of pleasure for me—not even a painful one... We split up, each worshipper going to a bare little chair, nothing more to it. Had I left my country, traveled so far, to wash up in this cave of little maniacs, fierce little listeners? I fell asleep, my feet hooked on the chair in front so I wouldn't fall over. Whenever I came to, they were still frozen there, as if forever, holding their breath, no sign shined for me, sleep on, sleep on. All through these séances I constantly dropped off and came to again, in the end only good for a bed—warm, flat and less Wagnerian. The first time, Wagner Girl let herself break in half in a murky street, slammed against my body, teeth chattering, froze for the longest time as if hypnotized, then let herself be led through her fatigue to the dawn. An angular body strung on an anxious melody, as the opening movement became naked candor in all four corners of the room, rhythmed to our hands' and mouths' insistence, thus the imposing overture to a song that became more and more tenor, then sshh! A silence with only the crack of the magic wand deciphering a few stray notes. The measured mildness of the second movement, between the cry of a bone and the diverting of a thigh, her body knotting and unknotting, earth kicked up in flight, then, in the empty brain pan, came the final movement in our symphony for a sealed room. The night bore on, my gaze was still clear, I was openly splitting in half.

Watering down the city like the many exiled nostalgias poured into it, I glided through Paris, relentless and unbowed, just a few indolent steps to find my selfsame glance in a miscellaneous café, my long fatigue, time's steady pace. You get the habit, in Paris, of living distraught, hardly one vague memory of nature. When water isn't one of the smells a city is only a space without enigma, uprooted from its farthest recollections. All is rendered sign there, the sign of being transparent to smoky meditations, seasonal butterflies of ideas, man's rendezvous—sum total of simulations.

I had just come through months of incomprehensible fatigue and suffering. Curled up against whatever was there, I slept wherever I could, a heavy sleep, and long; every now and again, at first detached in the real world, then substituted for the void, I plunged. Plus—what can you say about a sick man who lacks any illusion about his illness? The medical illusion is another thing altogether: Strain, he kept saying. Strain of what, and why? Everything waited to be confronted, beyond this endless sleep.

The first day was spent next to two well-liked people in a huge room full of sad, bourgeois trappings. The outside light came from the right, prolonged by the snow-cover, one window, a creaking snow, Stockholm, and sleep creeping forth when I'd barely found a seat. And perhaps I had followed the bright malicious smile of one woman, or the tousled hair of the other! That memory closes off a universe that isolated me in the softness of the chair, and behind this attitude of unbalanced voyeur (because, normally, I withdraw from groups before my own landscape can get torn), I was neither foreclosed identity nor someone fascinated by the fixedness of those beloved signs. By remembering, and reflecting, I see my body again, in the semi-circle, my legs straight out and parallel, the basic position for time's slowness whenever a part of me started to shift away; no surprise to be gained from the room, no startling of the nerves, just a displaced movement, the permutation of some wild number, and no nostalgic music coming back with it...

This was the beginning of a fatigue that at first I thought would pass, I put the whole world off to the next day. When it lasted, my will being the brother of its own bad luck, I withdrew into myself, rediscovered at the same time a ferocious appetite for reading. Though tired in body, I was not when it came to reading; this split saved me, I imagine. And so began the itinerary of a long year of convalescence between Morocco, Paris, Combloux and Stockholm.

117

There is nothing more wearying, and more depressing, than rest sanctuaries, places for man's worry expelled from among men through the treacherous mouthpiece of medicine, itself the sordid relative of universal poverty. There is no saving yourself in those isolated places where the suffering of people vomited by their familiars vegetates. Here, gentle reader, is the sad spectacle of arriving at Combloux. The air changes nothing, it disillusions you, the snow caused me suffering, I gobbled pills, gossiped with convalescents from every quarter. The doctor, a skeletal woman, gave me a dry hug, while going on about her family. A desert on the outside, and the inside too.

Luckily, I had found some living types, people whose presence among these ghosts I really couldn't understand. I met an Algerian on my first day, as I got off the bus. The snow was deep, the cold glacial. The sun gleamed. And that was all. But by the door of the chalet stood a boy with a rascal's gay air, in a formal suit but casual shoes. Surprised by this person, finding him misplaced, I said "You're crazy." He smiled and introduced himself. His deal was simple, he went cruising, day and night, in the affluent villages nearby. In between, he locked himself in; as a willing accomplice, I slipped him the key of the disco I was managing. Each morning, he would tell me his tales of the snow-bunnies, the women by ones and twos even, the piles of money from distant husbands, the pressing in bars, with lots of color and scent...

Both sexes rested in their separate chalets, you mixed during free time. I had a choice among several groups: the nutters (their own term) who worked themselves up dancing, the sickly intellectuals and many other bands, all hostile to my curiosity.

With a strange Vietnamese man and his sweet girlfriend, (after long discussions), we used to organize westerns on the snow. We had an abandoned cabin quite a ways off, to finish the minimalist movie of our escapism. We assassinated the snow, eliminated distance with our headlong races through the trees, and we fell, exhausted, incredibly happy, in front of a dilapidated old hearth. Yet again, childhood rediscovered, and its wildness.

They got us together once in a while for gloomy lectures, which always ended in a general uproar. I preferred taking care of my discotheque, music became my charity work.

I had those snowy mountains to take photographs of, absolutely pathetic, askew shots, my horizon continued to be inside me, my monologue as well, in the depths of a solitude that was increasingly sharp. And this is no simple flight between you and me, my reader, the act of imagining a snow butterfly who, to keep itself going, must not disintegrate in one direction or another, but instead move on according to the frightening harmony of its dividing. For, looking at that suffering now very long ago, I can find no sense except, at that time, my complete innocence about my own death.

Farewell, Left Bank and Paris of my adolescence. Difference is a woman and savage difference is a latent seduction. A fine illusion, returning to your own country! You can never go home, only fall back into the circle of its shadow. Yet, who was waiting for me? My mother, with wide eyes and the desire to transform everything.

I had acquired some knowledge, a dusting of psychoanalysis, a gravel-voiced sociology and a few smoky, poetic memories. My wife knew my country through the split images of my body. Our journey was about to begin, suspended in this double gazing: where did our identity end, and where spread the root of our tenderness?

What had I retained from this long stay of six years in Europe? A pointless question if you just hold on to the flight of it all. I talk about my past as if, each time, it was a matter of expelling a chunk of time. So be it! I give the floor to another double.

Adolescence came along, with its blossoming of little *clicks.* Going off in fascinations, scattered in the universe: seeing and getting to know everything, disappearing in advance into the notion of the voyage. I will have been far, in foreign countries, and I will have loved everything in that roving and its musical score.

Then what?

High Risk Series II

Fugue On Differentness

London displayed its balance, its precision, its mask; I walked with conviction, and though the asphalt might dream what a bounce I'd make, I wasn't at all repulsed by the grayish shapes, and their gradations from neighborhood to neighborhood in a way that made up a social circle. The strolling—among others—of a chance skirt of a certain pallor and flair. I had to move on and yet see; how was I to catch—beyond my prosody—that instant that tears itself open?

Treated the way travelers are everywhere, prisoners of their anonymous silence and adventure; like travelers throughout the world, my uncertainty was hard to wear down, no way to dominate everything at once: my breathing, my body's elocution, the gliding in a reality that lived inside my head, measuring my cigar, digressing, at the most it was all one witness's representation, a tribute to my overwhelming kind of attention.

To try to sketch out some internal motif, the beginnings of a bit of meditation, time, youth, vague mutterings of history, of the void, what was I supposed to be looking for in this city whose shifting differentness called attention to itself through the arbitrary, the obscurely arbitrary? People passed each other and quickly became shabby, I divided myself in parts, I went walking, I was sure, in complete innocence, that I could summarize myself to the city—my way of announcing my presence—beyond the museums and other old stuff.

Officially, I had nothing that I had to defend against my own indiscretion, maybe a side calculation, judging myself through their hints, in the silence of a street, varying

125

myself infinitely. Dance or invention? Telling myself, shyly evasive, that the animation in a local face, one that was smiling kindly, was just a paradox deferred. Them, they shed the memory—while keeping their masks, how could I assault them otherwise?—of a first performance that I had fled, a well-known and nonsensical interlude, since our mutual fainting spell was really a divining.

Seen from the back, we had the same way of swinging our feet while holding snapshot still, in a diaphanous transposition, whose outline lived in my room, despicable, really, inflicted on me by myself. Solitude was standing strong. Well! In the garden of the exiled I ate, slept well, read, my certainties all in a line, I watched over my swervings. Differentness, out the window with you!

Aside from all that, I had the impression of being acted, this minor identity that appeared unsimultaneous and squeezed forth from my lassitude, a life somehow orphaned, one that fancied itself unattached, light, innocent, penning impressions of English life to wife and friends.

I had observed, but your look tricks you; returning each time to your memory the thing has become attitude or ashes. And keep hold of what? Frightful identity, in that it suspends you between beats; falling back, fainting and memory-less, snatches of anecdote...

I was able to have, on the side, the risks of a little craziness at Round House, where, over two evenings, I mixed it up with this country's youth, youth I caught in gassy vignettes, jeans, well-read on the new and the fashionable, cruel haircuts, intervention of the old kif pipe, I changed myself by confusing myself with them, by corresponding; further on, a table with a poster of Che, cigar and genius, free delivery, retail ideology, you barter, buy a brochure, a prop, a few scratches on your bare feet, feathers, echoes, minor madness. I bent like a reed.

126

The program started right after my sandwich, grabbed just in time at the other end of the room. Up to the lectern came Stokely Carmichael, Allen Ginsberg and Laing, the psychiatrist, the least well-known, the craziest, unable even to get his mouth to behave. He erased the sexual revolution, or so he said, as his elbow slipped off the lectern—he couldn't completely topple over, the crowd, in its mercy, held him up, and what do we think about patient-psychiatrist relations in terms of the sexual revolution? Oppressed people everywhere, flail against the stars!

A very different thing, Allen Ginsberg's burbling, chanting a Chinese poem, but whose Chinese and made of what? The poet stuck out his pink tongue. They were all relaxing, these palpable men, all around me, shaken undefinably off in my personal distance. A Chinese poem, for which I'd gladly trade my delirium to this Occidental huckster. I was talking to myself, "Either the West or China!.." Over the course of the evening it was in fact a drugged Buddha that came back to me in the most highly wrought image. I was sad, even the lips of friends commenting on the events encouraged my distress. And now all was exaltation, Carmichael was speaking, "You, the English left, you confuse political liberation with liberation through drugs; I've been doing drugs since I was thirteen and I'm not free."

I suspected this magician of manipulating his breathing, of having a profound knowledge of this kind of thing; his rhythm broke down any resistance. You are the true, the beautiful, the only, the young horde shouted. An impostor of frank speech rose and, with a brief gesture, proclaimed to all that Carmichael was wearing Occidental pants. The scandal! –because the accused also wore an Indian tunic with gold threads. Carmichael insulted the man and left peacefully, the crowd was happy.

What came next was a Happening, black people in a black coach, piled one on another; legs over one another, let me act and then you will know, a type of theater, oh reader, ejaculated from what memory! Now a fluttering of calligraphy and perfumes. Going backwards a bit, by means of a one act play, characters separating to take each other on again, Hamlet must be here somewhere, I'm looking for him, alas! No more heroes, no more history, no more god, no more theater, nothing left but terrible voyeurs, staring each other in the face.

The evening's last composition, "The Social Deviants," a band spurred on by sociologists of the left. The party ended with everyone dancing, I worked out a few steps, and may one leg strain against another!

An isolated shout and I am suddenly elsewhere, my heart in my throat. Hello my good man, here is your route, no other way, talk to me when silence makes you despair. I could have passed, in that country, though unable to count my fingers. I look to the right, and pass by, I look to the left, and pass, with a mere gesture I pass, my breath scanned, in the last figure of dance. Shy when you say hello, violent when you're alone.

It was the city of Sofia in snow, and the entire tribe seeming to fear my gaze? Honorable creatures, remember my ransom, remember my sadness, should the Drunkenness of the Day of Great Violence arrive, a revolution against revolution, I will be poisonous from thinking about my lamentable absence.
Eating Bulgarian or Turkish style became a reasonable plan, on the menu I would point to the cucumbers in yoghurt, same dish, same objections, honorable creatures!

One image of happiness among these people, at the main theater of Sofia, a refreshing change for me, because my interpreter was slipping in his own commentary, which created two unintelligible texts on that distant stage. The main character picked himself up, mustache drooping, fatty drool, vomit; with his breast-plate of blood, I could see the omen coming. Bourgeois, the interpreter whispered, bourgeois...

They were laughing all around me. The bourgeois character was indeed humiliated, but I, oh socialist realism, I was already dozing off! In a cloud I saw the play unfold: the bourgeois guy, making a pass at the servant, put some gold in her cleavage. His wife showed up just at that moment; in her plump goodness, she let herself be rolled. Curtain for the first act.

During intermission they filled my ears some more, I dreamed about the faces filing by, had I got the century, and the mirror, wrong? Already disoriented by my cramped legs, I settled into these new tidings. Time, my goodbye, my roaming, cannot erase the poor beggar that I was, wanting only one object, a single object on the other side of the veil.

Indani Rajpai Rahman! You were dancing, I was coming from afar, there is your first movement, still an obsession; may distance be torn, and may those perish who have no memory, down to the last man! I came from afar, an airy melody, several stopovers, capitals piled one on another, I saw nothing, and then I was in India, people of my savage difference.

I arrived late at night. An Afro-Asia conference, but who cares. I take off, pleasure lies elsewhere in that land. In the evening you dance, you turn your hands palm out, and here are other ethereal signs, your fingers as in a dream, crossing over, balance, a balance that The Day of Great

Violence will shatter into echo. Your hands draw near me; in their dance I read, recite, write my own parable. And I ask of your fingers what I do not grasp, I split in two, I am your movement, I soar away, come back, a pact between you and me, letter of all letters, a final and painful graph that makes me sleep through the night at my hotel, projected against the calligraphy of desire.

You went on dancing around me, while I went about in the city, an inhabitant only by signing, and *snick!* I grab a match, and, surrounded by so much misery, I light up and proclaim that the sign burst forth, Indani Rajpai Rahman!

Far off is the cave where, in the center, hides that image hitched to sunrise, and to sunset. I was coming down the mountain, or maybe going up it, a minor deception if you accept the men who came after me. And one day, I will return among them, The Day of Great Violence!

Your descent, says the Koran, is a word only, rapid as the blink of an eye.

In the middle of the square, in a village of the Atlas region, the popular festival made me think of the pages about Abraham, my own irresistible throat-slitting and the water battles in the neighborhood of my youth. A masked festival, rams' heads hung on rags, wrenched about to the rhythm of a baton. Approach, people, all here is magic and clouds, approach! The masks came forward, cursing the cursed races. Why was I struck still before this dance? A breath, a word only, prompt as the blink of an eye.

If I had had the keys of the city, ancestral Cordoba! If I were poetry, fallen princes, ruins, frescos, mosques! I had always been the son of my father and his father, I foresaw neither paradise nor enigma that my feet might have trampled. My brother wandered in those deserts of beautiful memory, seeking a trace of his Andalusian forebears. Now Andalusia breathed with another fury.

The same heat as in Marrakesh, the same illusion of your chest being wide open, I wandered in the labyrinths, getting closer, irresistibly, to my form. A place, a myth, a crossing.

That night, "Fuck fuck lady," I asked of a child who seemed to drill into my past. He and I, the look-alike child who spoke confidentially, as well as outside the two of us, his hands in his pockets, and me, father of a child and also of a childhood, keeping certain signs firm and distant, due to my divided book, signs that were tipping towards death. No money, said the Spanish boy, no woman, nothing, the tourist gets turned on, big or small, only wants to know the way.

I made my gesture, he made another, turning his hand over, pouting. My shadow, one, two, three, and wheeling on a street corner. I gave the boy a cigarette; between him and my childhood came the same song of the ocean: the *click* that came with the wave. He knew everything, for sure, I paced the neighborhood. Someone pointed, we stopped, knocked, they offered me the sex of a grinning, wild-haired forty-year-old to munch. The second floor was far off, hard to open the door, he—a wry grin, hands in pockets—and me, advancing, pulled along. No way to shatter that mirror, climb out, mass grave, misery, the old misery, and at the door the mother of that day's whore, a toothless bat who pulled me by the pocket: Give it to me, now go in! Grandmother, nothing more for you, beat it, I have thirty-two teeth but only dust to eat. The boy was waiting outside, me up in a bed wedged near the ceiling, had to feel around, gulp in the heat, legs, one, two, three and bang! –for spreading as well as spread, emptied down to my fingertips, I prolonged, come what might, my body's draining. Wisely, the whore rounded up my cock's

131

number, a rip in the void, nothingness, Spain humiliated, I would have settled for trading my fatigue and my long walk to get free, if only in the despair of such an old misery, one that came back to me through that child-like smile, this woman left to fuss with her clothes. The old woman was still at the door, I was already beyond her, hurtling down the stairs. Slightly cooler outside; at the corner of a street the boy showed me the way. We walked along laughing.

I had long ground my teeth about Spain, because I hated bullfights, but luckily I dream of the flamenco dancer's panting when desire overtakes me, and it takes me further than my own breath.

No plans that day, walking in the Jardin du Luxembourg, strolling, pacing near the children around the sailboat pool, children escaping their watchers, not yet strangled by neckties, seeing the branch waver, then disappear, walking through the people in chairs, around my own steps, my own disconnectedness, advancing over and above so many little slips in my own risks, so much distance in my own breathing in all the disjointed brushing-by. That's how my feet ventured forth. I sketched out the distance, lodged in a memory that was less and less nomadic, and, instead of tipping into visibility, I decided to angle off to a corner of the park I didn't know.

She turned around, I turned in the abyss, she turned around again, this girl in a black coat, a memory easily discarded if that chance fear hadn't beguiled me, exceeding me, and lengthening my distance, a double gazing where I thought some theater might lurk, miniaturized and shocking. On checking the faces of some old couples, at the mercy of their benches, hats pulled down to their ears, I fell into a silence with no return, and what happened was I stared at them for a few seconds, at that moment certain of my glacial eternity. Here they are, dead, here I am, dead, I move on, bowed. No doubt she thought I begrudged her chest or her words, hurried as she seemed in the permutations of our little enterprise. We were both stopped by a woman's cry, as she was hit by a car. Everyone froze. Our game was over, as our gaze had found its limit. Stretched on her back, the groaning woman fixed her dress with one movement, and a movement so full, so loaded by the many centuries, by so many breasts borne on golden platters, so many nightmares drowned in blood and books. This fleeting movement, which, in normal life, counter-balances seduction, came back to me later in a strangely provoking way; she might have died, her hand guarding her crotch.

A passerby jumped in, did that same gesture over again, pulling her dress straight several times, then tried to evaluate the whole accident. No wounds from mere looking, beware of invisible crusades, no blood, my fellow pleasure-seekers!

I was already distracted, vaguely meditative: Was the Christian West embodied in that movement? No betraying yourself in the face of death, maintaining the strength of your convictions, tying yourself up in suffering in such a way that life divides the signs and their meanings in a veiled madness. Still, I recognized the parallel spectacle of my identity, and, though drifting in the wilderness of the gods, I felt a certain emotion, the page's whiteness charming my distance from all the occidents of my prairie, birds strangled at my hand, unruliness of fingers. Open your hand and pass on!

Let the spring be all violet! The snow goes slowly away—in memory, anemone blue—as if pushed away by the former grass. A revealing of signs that have come back through the robin's song, through ice breaking, a sound

133

not amiss, but explicit in this diaphanous waking. Let the spring be all violet!

I knew the way the seasons chained together in that country, forests with changing colors according to that drumbeat. I think of my right hand, almost frozen in the snow, as I was coming down the mountain, heedless of my own height. That day, however, I was far from my past. In Stockholm, I'm sure at this season of the year of not mistaking this person's hair—believing, as I do, that my wife's blondness is the very scent of my difference. We were walking, perhaps hand in hand, towards another possibility. Young couples passed with armfuls of flowers.

A Swedish melody led me straight to the modern art museum, and to Nana of Niki Saint Phallus, or some such thing. You may recall that enormous sculpture of a woman with vagina open to the visitor. For today, let's not bother staring at paintings, like perverts. Not the twinkling of an eye, rather your hand on the first floor landing of the uterus. Shy when you say hello, violent when alone. And how could she have had a kid when no mortal had ever touched her, this saint Nana? How might I have burnished my flesh in that crack, and who can accuse me of dying, living, dying, living to the rhythm of my suffering?

Fashionable foundation for a paradise, and transposition to a lovers' bench, whose every word, we're told, was sucked up by a hidden microphone. We strolled in single file, beer and sandwiches. And now you change from day to day without mixing up your fables. Here you live, hands in pockets, at the heart of the ephemeral word, and may the few rare analogies disguise themselves from their lovely death!

In crossing through so much fog and confetti, no mother is found, oh Swedish rhetoric whose foreign grimace still surges up in me! Even if my identity stayed transparent, could I register myself, numberless, in this sex organ, while rebounding from my vast fever?

Now nothing looked like my divinings, I split in two from afar, with little movements in the leaves, an unsteady wink, neither uprooted nor in a flash of lightning, a touching, with no outburst against the cruelty of desire. To veer against your own shadow in this arbitrary country. I cite not only the displacement of signs, a pleasure that comes back to me through woods and snow, a sweetness never removed by any refusal, not only my body—a talisman signaled in the course of my wandering. Say it now: I give and receive, so many birds fall silent without my knowing. Can I ever be blind to anonymity and fasten myself to rhythm?

We debased ideology under other skies, as usual, I was coming from far away, a little weary, but the first morning had me floating in cigar smoke. Speech—itself burgeoning in this international colloquium, clamped onto passions, to order—circulated in this convulsing of different peoples who stiffened with every breath. Man was new again, so said the narrative, though I felt the suffering in it, man against the doubling of time that binds any revolution.

I fled the lovely speech, artificial when desire begins to smolder, to find Havana whose emptiness of street and commerce of color kept changing before my eyes; behind it all, there was plant life exotic enough to hold me suspended, and the joy of children possessing the street like a toy. At nightfall, too, I moved about in a flight of colors, toward the university square, where there was dancing. The olive seller, an irresistible black woman—plus I was going away for a long time. In that land, no rutting lewdness, but simple truth without the anxious-to-please look or gesture. Spineless traveler, say it now: I only seize truth thanks to the expansion of so many

135

equations sprung from a single dance step, say it: let them dance, those who dance! what now! what! Let yourself go a bit, invertebrate dancer. I was smoking a fat cigar, and nothing to be proud of!

Never turn your back to the dagger, but say, "Hi," face to face, keeping your distance! Measure time with a simple glance, with the flare of good news. In the wilderness confront the hyena's deceit face to face. Say, "The hyena's flesh resembles the donkey's, same smell, same problem, my brothers." Smash its head, the fount of all divining, walk without trembling; if his liquid, following tradition, catches you afraid, he will follow you till you die, soon one morning you are but desert bones. You will have no place, poor poet, in the cemetery by the near sea, a cemetery of wood, wrecks carved with the sign of the female camel and the tribe's genealogy. Stop the gazelle at the threshold of the ocean, caress her from afar and let her race on the beach. Say: I am dying of mad passion and I've lost the veil, trying to reach passion's wings; say: my pen flies away at the shock of the sand ruins, and may the earth tremble! May The Day of Great Violence arrive! Avoid that desert snake that only bites once, crush it for all time beneath the rock, dance with all your power before it makes you dance. Perhaps you will have the power of blood, the eye being mortal, yea though the night goes on into night. Perhaps you will pitch your tent on firm ground, a sleep between the hyena and the stars.

Well, what now! does he, the guest of the desert, believe he can play with this space and run no risk for his own space? What! does this guest believe he can wander better than the desert, and in his wandering what words will hold him back from this void that gives nothing back? And what! can he bound back through centuries with the

136

Bedouins, towards the horde of poets stabbed in the back, an old parchment's kingdoms and pens made from reeds?

Three pigeons fall with one arrow, the hand opens at just one rhyme and Antar—the Arab bard—lopped off a thousand heads to make desire take root in the last grass blade. Step into the parable when you say "Hello" to Bedouins. Be free with your gesture—give it with your best wishes. Say hello a hundred times without getting the courtesies wrong. Tell no lie in the long litany, repeat until all is sworn. Men will offer you camel's milk, women will fall in behind you. Stop with any tribe, hold to your pride among peers, pray, greet and listen!

There you are, now, among true Bedouins. You observe the scant wheat and small flock. The tribe's chief says, "Divide the grains of wheat in so many grades, three grains for the chief's beard, and one grain each among all the equals. Where rain falls once a year, once and that's it, share the drops like so many grains, also leaving their share for equals far away, betray not the absent, for the absent one is also the desert. Do not steal, even alone and unveiled, and if you steal, offer your hand to be severed. The desert has long watched ghosts like you; they will break apart, it is written, in this vast silence."

I recite all these formulas to myself and go off, the desert will not totter, and I will have only sand in my teeth.

Have a smoke with the fishermen you meet, wait, that's what the desert is, an immense waiting. Say it: granted, I have come, but what have I done? I have ventured outside myself, but what have I done, recited, read, written? May the great departure soon come!

You will cross desert towns half submerged, Tan-Tan, Tarfaya, tents of concrete, push them out of your way. At the limit of your fatigue you will arrive in a circular garden, you will glide up to the gate formed by two bent

137

stakes. Perhaps you can count the rare seed spikes, perhaps you will find inebriation and a brutal abundance; you will know to find, at the bottom of a tiny pot, just two branches of mint, branches so small that all your fire will go into dreaming. Perfumes! Calligraphy!

Haunted by the kilometers of that carpet, which kept with me till I got to my room. Cool air on condition, sir. Here the turbans stalk you in the corridor and a strange odor forces you to flee. As an adolescent, I used to dream of India as of an aroma from my loftiest recall. The same multifarious speech in one more international colloquium.

Fleeing New Delhi for Delhi, itself a tireless scattering. I excuse myself for leaving, hardly worth the price of this disturbance. I settle in behind the young driver, a bicycle for us two, his heaving form divides my gaze in half, I bump up against an extreme slow motion, turning around the slightest point in space, a panting where my conciliations become muddled. Not just Gandhi's sanctuary, open to good news, but that tenderness and nakedness face to face, he who knew the economy of silence, even further than death. Agra? Taj Mahal? Throw out this glacial eternity and all the third rate gods. Come down from your refuge, walk, cross the street, that grocer surrounded by matches and candles stares at you from behind a shadowy veil, a man so frightfully thin. Howl like a child and pass on!

One cry and I find myself elsewhere, my heart in my throat. Hop in, hello, sir, here is your path between the two cities. They prepare you for the shock. Here they show the victims of the wall, photos of heroes beyond the barbed wired, flowers and smiles, all escaped through a keyhole, all craftsmen of a little death. I owe them nothing, they owe me nothing, and I move on, head bowed.

Berlin right or left, what does it matter! Just latch on to the force of the image, in West Berlin industrious shamelessness, stores vegetating in the splendor; by evening the neon with thirty stars, a few whores to light the whole thing up. No stable ground, cut prices, capitalism, one step back, two steps into the void and I move on.

Climbing the wall from curiosity, here lies the dog ever watching, here lies the grenade that catches you as you jump, in the very heart of history. Perched a few meters from East Berlin, meditate a little while, in the West they tell you: we are one people; they also tell you: he looks like me, that person walking there, brother in wall and war, that identical being, maybe he also has a gray coat and a cold face, maybe a man, maybe less, when close up you insist on it, and the wall fades away. Atrocious image of this paradise!

Go to the East, appear from the other side, you'll see. A customs man below ground aims me the right way, nothing to it, a slipping on into the other city, stores and a café like anywhere, nothing comes back to me, no war, no grimace. Exiled in my own ideology for an afternoon I become weary. Farewell, Berlin wall, undo yourself and fall down!

Travels or dancing? My roaming among all these peoples—and one day I'll recapture its interferences again, face to face—an interminable fascination whose signs I renounce, and what fable could retell my movements? Furtive exchange, a whim, an equation of visions that make me drift—where differences meet—toward my own divining.

Recall those Cuban children possessing their neighborhoods like toys, chessboard of rhymes and colors, and may the becoming of The Day of Great Violence, far beyond my breath, explode in their crystalline malice!

Variation on Differentness

Hey now! Hey! Paris, the haunting madwoman, and oh my soul was fragile! I hadn't followed the immemorial advice: when you come into a town without being able to speak to anyone, repeat a hundred times oh Usher, repeat a hundred times oh Savior, repeat a hundred times oh Merciful of all the Merciful Ones, all creatures will then advance toward you, by divine edict. Hey! Hoo!

At the end of the parable there was the same vacant lot of culture, my eyes were open in the heart of the idolater France and I was saying: Occident, you have torn me apart, you have ripped out the pit of my thinking. Occident, I will stretch out your alabaster body, really, for real, nothing more, nothingness of nothing, nothing. I will lay it out on a tree trunk, with the jiggling of my right hand, held just at the tear in your dress. Hey! Hey now! The wind will come by, really, for real, over your hips and their betraying movements, a gust! because my right hand, taken up by harmony, by trance, inverts your caress, and the same hand undresses you facing the sun. Hey! Holy culture,—bah!—make me an enigma among the horde of beggars, wake up and expel my tribal blood, and may I eat of my brother's flesh!

Occident, on your blond hair, blond as I want and desire it, and the same string at the center of words, tumble down! tumble down, memories, and dear Madame High Art... tumble, ambrosia of blond hair, nectar, who knows who makes the other bow down: God or the rooster or the earth?

Swallow your vipers, Occident, your stones erected. Be man, be woman! I dwell in your gaze, I take the boat, glide into the river, upright birds, childhood—ploop!—I glide some more, saved in a waking dream on an island of tamarisk and bitter fruits, perhaps a stork, a queen's ring,

141

evening falls and the glint assassinates its stars. The silence of a madman, nothing more, nothingness of nothing, nothing! What island, oh Occident, have you found for your savages? And your ass with its tricolor flag, as my friend said, heh heh! Heh!

Once arrived in your gaze I am dispossessed of my *One Thousand and One Nights*, nothing more to say, I have the parchment in my pocket, and even better—*The Book of Songs,* hey now! Hey! A very beautiful queen once loved a poet, whom she let into her bed in the absence of the honored king. She next put him in a chest, clack!,. dropped him through a trap door. One day the servant catches them between bed and trap door and informs the king, who, as sly as he was furious, comes in to hold forth in a poetic vein about the apparent disorder of the furniture. He points out the chest on which the queen was sitting, before her prayers, "Two prostrations before Love, with ablutions to be done in blood." They talk back and forth without rage, through rhyme and through death, and, suddenly seized by a rigid spasm, right there they understand all, and, looking as though nothing is happening, they start talking about the stars. The servant takes the chest, nobody dares look at it, and drops it down a well, plop! one poor poet in the coolness of song.

Certainly, Occident, I split in two, but my identity is an infinity of interplay, of sand roses, euphorbia is my mother, desert is my mother, oasis is my mother, I am protected, oh Occident!

You have opened up to the rhythm of relaxation, yoga right and left, fakir with infinite member stretching from heaven to earth, cathedrals! Can you perk up your breasts without betraying yourself, are you the pit and not the flower? In the history I learned my tribe had so many poets, all great, all struck down from behind, blind,

142

thieves, assassinated on a stretch of sand, one destiny shared by signs and daggers.

In my history, there were two poets of opposite peoples and sexes. She sends a message so that truth will burst forth; fearful, he seeks advice at great length, an elder offers this enigma: there is no conquest of the universe without symbol, he says. Our prophet pitches an immense tent, whips up a basin of water, perfumes of every description, crystal, brocade and satin. The other prophet arrives so that truth may burst forth, the drunkenness of truth. He receives her at the door, says hi to her, has her come in, recites a short and decisive poem. Then the prophetess's body opens up when the perfume mixes with the water. Hey! Hey-oh!

On your stomach, Occident, I delay the end of all ends, my revenge of smashing everything, wellspring and fetus, shooting and dying, the barbaric differentness, and I'll go instead to the nodal point, to wear down your resistance, your rest. I have chosen, it's obvious yet unclear, seduction and a distant will. What have I to fear in your abduction, dear Occident?

I have dreamed an irreversibility, beyond the wounding bristle, for I fall in full vengeance on your belly; whoever wants to grasp either knowledge or the orifice must provoke—face to face—that multiple veil, that abduction, one step back, two steps in the void, nothing, nothingness of nothing, nothing more.

My right hand timed to this moratorium, everywhere the Berber parable starts up again: "Desire is like a son. Even were he blind or lame, could you forget him?" No abstinence, and why, why? I am not jealous of my own brothers, the ones offered to paternal memory, and I, the son of two mothers or Becoming's lover, bah! They have seen, Occident, on your chest, the sign of your curse, occidental syphilis they declared it, the syphilis of frightened differentness, and on your breasts, they went on to declare, your death is carved, for God is great and all the rest is negligible. What's more true than that? Bah!

I am not jealous of my brothers, nor of my fathers. In truth, Occident, when everything crumbles in our embrace, I'm already thinking of the day of destruction. May it come, The Day of Great Violence!

I pin your hips to the sand, I curl your body against the explosion of escape and I wait: all this happens out beyond the spices, the cry of childhood.

On your vulva, my Occident, I tattoo the calligraphy of our infidelity, a fire at the tip of each finger. The nodal point, *crrack!*

Double versus Double
(Dialogue)

FIRST IMAGE

A. –Listen to me without betraying, or else go, go accuse the wind.

B. –I'm listening, I do betray you. You recount your childhood, you take us on the tour of your little life—which has nothing special about it, you have to admit. But perverse as you are, sly as you think you are, you lump your downfall together with signs, you yank back your hand when history gives you a hard time: a syllable here, a vowel there, and childhood, plop!

A. –Poor lost soul! Though I'm the demoted son of my father, I desire—but, desire, will you ever get this?—to make you feel the necessity of my inheritance. I have often said that my being is not this void that you suggest, this black eye where I might lose myself in mortal fascination, even if in the depths of the pupil there is the fear of being devoured by a bit of tobacco smoke, as, drifting back towards my fatigue, it wraps and disappears in my own flesh. Let's suppose this void is, in a flash, irrevocable—isn't it true that the memory of it is pure erasure? You can start at any point and all the rest is chance, at each moment its memory can be gained or destroyed, once and for all, in an unconfessed fraud.

B. –I remember all that, and I remember your illusions when it all seems to come down to a goat's caper.

A. –Well now! The disillusionment (and it's no longer for sale) was one of the century's hypotheses, shared by many writers, while as for me, I shatter myself between day and night, no place to drop where I might suppose my current identity is wrapped up, not a void, not a nostalgia for so many gods, but the knot between two voids, or, as I picture it, the knot of my Great Violence, that would spread incandescence and death from both edges. The knot of my earliest story, which I would also claim as my final story, if fear didn't hold me back.

B. (*smiling*). –Your derision, madness, books!

A. (*after stopping a moment*). –Let's suppose this hypothesis of disillusion doesn't exist, then that would put me somewhere, between you and me, division and rhythm, dialogue between the sea and my childhood, and possessed by my double identity—by my culture as well as the West—, revolving in the very interior of my mask...

B. (*still smiling*). —?

A. (*with a wink*). —Remember Muhammad—the prophet of no written words—, remember his cave, his desultory meditation. What words, what incantation, what breath? He let himself be carried about, and spoken for, by a multitude of palpitations, it was his women, his friends or his tribe that wrote down his inspiration.

B. (*obscurely shaken*). –I agree to latch on to your innocence.

A. –In this sense, we are suggesting that behind my childhood there is no special and immemorial inspiration that I bring, with cleverness or fetishism, to your awareness. It matters little to me if history deteriorates...

146

B. (*furious*). –Fill me in on your current identity rather than your rhyming prose and all your divinings. Nothing to be done with your fetishes— *becoming* is my position. Everything is holding firm. (*He opens the window and looks out.*)

A. (*his eyes still very jumpy*). –It matters little to me that this inspiration deteriorates in the parchment, the Koran or other books. Maybe you'll understand one day, but what day might that be, what day? Perhaps this timeless memory will turn my disorder upside down, but the whole century is crazy. Crazier than my joy, when I tremble alone.

B. – The truth is, my friend, I have chosen, I allow myself to live... (*pulling himself together*): Thinking all these things you think, what a rout for your idea of final knowledge!

A. (*his gaze suddenly attracted by the image of a woman tattooed on the background of a Chinese fresco, an image capable of swallowing appearances, including the characters A and B*). – Let's admit it, in a roundabout way, that the whole horde of signs doesn't disturb the goat's leap, or, if you prefer, that music doesn't disturb knowledge. It suggests, on the contrary, its veiled dialectic. Disharmonious thinking doesn't interest us. (*Silence.*) Are you listening?

B. (*facing outside*). –Your movements could be reversed. (*Also remembering the tattooed woman*): From the lower lip to the slope of the chin, a black line and four black dots, the separation of woman, you had come no doubt with the dagger, running from far away, from behind the wave.

A. –What a strange country, where childhood opened up to the sun, the very heart of my recall, ideas soon escaped from their nest, what a strange country! Let's start up again as parable.

B. (*fascinated by his right hand, which had slowly withdrawn from the other—and visibly moved*). Brother of my father's father!

A. (*with his gaze returned to the photo*). –Although the cry from that childhood spares my health, the enigma to decipher—freely as long as we stay on this deserted shore—sends us back to that knotted identity. May that strange country step towards us, we said! If its representation really takes shape, we will have borne witness to our reflection in history, through our precipitous descent against the Occident. Enigma upon enigma, we were wont to take this contemporary Occident for a wound. And just at that moment she arrived, the veiled woman. Recall her hands and their tracery of henna,, remember her protection, her mildness, her myths, her whimsical tales. Also remember the sound of the sea.

B. –No flight of barbaric birds could unbind our tenderness.

A. –In such a way first graphic sign, then echo, then scent...

B. (*furious*). –What an identity, cobbled together that way!

A. (*looking at the photo of the woman, now bare of tattoo*). –An extremely diaphanous identity that alighted just there, where scents are recalled, such is her destiny forever, an identity beneath which nothing is reflected, only the maternal fiddle-bow, or immemorial song of the sea. Who has ever been able to usurp, by force or by death, the final sign? Upon this question, even if you uproot it from its

148

frightfulness, what a flowering of miserable differences!

B. (*violently*). –Difference is your own word.

A. –If you wish.

B. –Ungraspable in your folly, you will suffer in body and mind—there's no way to disconnect identity and differentness. Know this!

A. You think you can make me trip at one end or the other of the knot, I am alive, divided in all different ways. To get you to argue more merrily, might we demonstrate in all calmness the wanderings of history? Could we ever separate out its gamut or its contradictions without a paralysis of signs? Really, it's enough to produce, for a time at least, a few crazed identities, history will do the rest, that's its job, a few identities that are crazy and yet far removed from the Great Violence. As long as you can always save your neck. What would we make of a theater without actors? Thus we dream, from you across to me, through the disillusioned distance; because of this scene that's immediately forgotten, we conclude that differentness, like identity, is a rhythm and a painful dance. Perhaps we will be shown mercy on this first point.

SECOND IMAGE

A. −Truly...
B. (*he tears himself violently from the window and comes back toward the shadow of A, hopping*). −In bringing back a dead enigma from our evanescence, you think you can detail, in the dancing arithmetic of concepts, an equally obscure plot, your very own circularity that you interrupt to your own advantage, convinced that the universe is after you. Can we ever willingly accept the way words wander over a knot of meaning, one that shifts and doesn't shift? The kind of movement that's possible when writing confronts the general madness of signs.
A. (*flapping his hands*). −In truth, who, among all my parallels, will echo me? (*eyes closed*): Can you shock me on this point?
B. (*ironic*). −Perhaps you're all alone in disguising yourself with such glory?
A. (*gaze fixed on the window, a goat leaps*). −Even if the symbolic woman we're talking about positively rolls in henna and they take a whip to me, I am sure I can resist any dividing, me, the colonized-decolonized intellectual. (*Silence.*) With this gesture of the fear that colors our lives, we regain rightfully—not despairingly—the lone possibility: to come down though yourself, in your double identity or, if you prefer, to revive the pure blossoming of the signs, in an agitation of aggression or love. In this way the body reinforces itself, you can laugh it off, and what do knowledge or failure matter! Otherwise, identity must teeter in

a vacant zone or in pure nostalgia. That resolves nothing in itself, and what solution could be possible, what a question, brother of my father's father? That touches upon the chessboard of evanescences that we used to cite while turning them back, to their downfall, which above all does take place. (*Shaking his head.*) In this event which defines exaltation, we deduce the swerving of our identity on the stage.

B.   –Always believing a choice is possible, between a dive into identity or its void or its madness, and an exact dancing in the fury of words—other theaters being superfluous.

A.   –Well then! Whatever implications there are in an identity, it's not a question—from everything we've seen—of gazing at yourself in this play of mirrors. They can have it, those who like this little game of circling-back-again! It is indeed a question of violence, in a scheme that's increasingly complex, to the point that...

B.   –What violence? What scheme? (*folding his hands*).

A.   Let's stick strictly to the truth, this scheme only stands out in the pure blossoming of signs. Take for example, if our demonstration is going to hold water, the tattooing of another cry on my being, a cry whose discourse we try to feel out, or whose dissonance, or even more, whose link to desire—a cry that speaks to my being and ruffles the parable down to its very stem. From Mohammed's cave to the air we now breathe, you have to admit the desert makes itself heard...

B.   –By people—in every era—who believe in levitating tables!

A. (*calmer*). –At the same time we can admit that Koranic parable can't be easily reconstituted for perverse goals, it shapes the memory of an identity, which learning can replicate in some current rhetoric or other—our book. In this battle, we try to save the image of a child, a finished thing, a buried thing, that above all takes place, the book, the starting point of the series of parallels. It still bears the stamp of another rhythm.

B. (*furious*). –Whether the cave holds up or not, were we imaging all the crossing of identities and differences in the pure dream of the sign? We admit that the Occident fascinated us unto death, that we have been divided unto death, a death whose metamorphosis one should not facilitate, our breath is to be sent to the mountain, and parable to the talisman. Out beyond, you'll traffic in mirages. For me, it all holds together because the body is within and without. Know this!

A. (*comes back to the window, notices the shadow of a man on the ground, his head bloody*). –So it appears we pass each other in a chance flash, in which I ally myself to the evanescence above and below cited. Let's go back to talking in parables. (*Outside, vague shiftings of a crowd through the dust; celebration or war?*)

(A.)   History is our desire, tied—like any other desire—to the violence of time. Let us divide our current vision of the present into little signs; may tattooing—the first sign—initiate me into memory; may scents—the second sign—open enigmas for me; may calligraphy—the third sign—open also the Koran that supposes my childhood, and, through these three little signs, may the Great Violence be heard as echo—that is what will surely arrange our

152

disposition. Though we used to wish that history would soar on its own wings, now we know enough about it to annul those legends of the void and the world, to take up parable there where we have discussions among the goats. It seems we have lived through the initial decomposition of a parchment, which was our father's and history's. All the while thinking I was parchment, and hoping, in my factual being, for its relative shrewdness, a fraudulent shrewdness, to be sure, but one which derived from the resonance of childhood and ended up sharpening the tension between words, justifying the resistance of that knot.

B. –Flights of fancy only upset the demonstration. Have you gauged its fragility?

A. –I think, in fact, that the primal source whose dizzying hypotheses we've brushed up against is well beyond the maternal fiddle-bow, it is not a question of a line traceable in our thought between identity and difference, rather a simple line that you can make travel with your breath, with your open chest, and inscribe in distended temporality, preferably stretching between our interchangeability and the cry yet to come. An image, then, that makes us come back, through the centuries, to the contradictory scent lodged between the primal source and insane time. At that point all is decided.

B. (*tender*). –Brother of my father's father!

A. –Well now! Seal yourself onto my fluttering or die, fake image of myself. Would I triumph over your mask if I split myself up forever? Woe unto those who are alone and tremble not. Perhaps we will be shown mercy on this second point.

153

FINAL IMAGE

After that celebration, or war, person B jumps into the Chinese fresco which now changes color; outside the goat hangs from the argan tree. Out past the crowd, the ocean hesitates in its surge. Facing the window, Person A, exalted, says:

Greetings, nonetheless, my guests of the day and my blood brothers. Rather than history in parables, the century holds other disorders, war and misery. Stop this sliding into pure divining. It will be said that I will come again among you, in the form I take after life has gotten to me. Well then! We will do nothing that abandons the meaning of history. It has been said: history is unique, it is identity, mad identity, it has neither engendered nor been engendered, equal unto itself. I lay the word before you. Have I not gathered around my eyelash the dreams of your deliverance? Behold my eyes, behold my hands. Have I not made of my body a restless and inexhaustible amusement? When will the word belong to all, oh my guests of the day? Woe unto him who breaks down without snatching death from death! Woe unto him who looks you up and down without trembling. Who will teach you to stand tall? Beware of him who traffics one message for another. What then! Will you betray my childhood and the source of your power? What is happening to you? Have I not given unto you the key to your long nightmare, when what you asked of me was good news—what are you doing? What are you doing that I will not do? When I dance before you, oh Occident, without dispossessing myself of my people, know that this dance is one of mortal desire, oh maker of haggard signs. Thus will it be for me and mine. The West believes in its power—think, oh my

154

guests of the day, even if your thought is mortal; the West can live, so live against your nightmare, far beyond your breath; it can die, be vigilant to the point of cruelty. Be vigilant! It has said: the universe is our abode. Answer it: may all abodes crumble, and may the day of Great Violence arrive as a strange echo. Strike at it, face to face! Otherwise, hand yourself over and collapse. Say: we are our own direction, we are our own movement. The Occident traded you for its own negation. Refuse these alms, refuse all alms!

In truth, we have said enough. Perhaps we will be shown mercy for all this parchment.

Postface

Being a high-rank wrestler in "the tribe of words," that original plan—autobiography and meditation—has transformed itself into a little novel with several voices, and finally into a theatrical work. There it *becomes*, it seems to us, putting into practice a circular distress, in order to get us through the checkpoints of history, to play upon history with a tension between pre-established language and the manuscript to come.

This recounted life is far from exemplary, no doubt. Let's accept the idea that writing about oneself is putting oneself forth as an emotional spectator or a terrorist—reason enough, for some people, to go through an uncertain therapy. Literary tinkering displaces this fascinated gaze upon self, moves it toward a clash of doubles, doubles derived from an illusion and as if drawn into a geometric complexity—writing.

Frightening autonomy of words, which, deployed about the body and the world, know how to betray, no use looking for shelter! So that the last page of the book becomes separation.

Tattooed memory—the book's title—is by way of dedication to my mother. Decolonizing yourself of what? Of insane identity, insane differentness. I'm speaking to all people.

L'HARMATTAN ITALIA
Via Degli Artisti 15; 10124 Torino
harmattan.italia@gmail.com

L'HARMATTAN HONGRIE
Könyvesbolt ; Kossuth L. u. 14-16
1053 Budapest

L'HARMATTAN KINSHASA
185, avenue Nyangwe
Commune de Lingwala
Kinshasa, R.D. Congo
(00243) 998697603 ou (00243) 999229662

L'HARMATTAN CONGO
67, av. E. P. Lumumba
Bât. – Congo Pharmacie (Bib. Nat.)
BP2874 Brazzaville
harmattan.congo@yahoo.fr

L'HARMATTAN GUINÉE
Almamya Rue KA 028, en face
du restaurant Le Cèdre
OKB agency BP 3470 Conakry
(00224) 657 20 85 08 / 664 28 91 96
harmattanguinee@yahoo.fr

L'HARMATTAN MALI
Rue 73, Porte 536, Niamakoro,
Cité Unicef, Bamako
Tél. 00 (223) 20205724 / +(223) 76378082
poudiougopaul@yahoo.fr
pp.harmattan@gmail.com

L'HARMATTAN CAMEROUN
BP 11486
Face à la SNI, immeuble Don Bosco
Yaoundé
(00237) 99 76 61 66
harmattancam@yahoo.fr

L'HARMATTAN CÔTE D'IVOIRE
Résidence Karl / cité des arts
Abidjan-Cocody 03 BP 1588 Abidjan 03
(00225) 05 77 87 31
etien_nda@yahoo.fr

L'HARMATTAN BURKINA
Penou Achille Some
Ouagadougou
(+226) 70 26 88 27

L'HARMATTAN SÉNÉGAL
10 VDN en face Mermoz, après le pont de Fann
BP 45034 Dakar Fann
33 825 98 58 / 33 860 9858
senharmattan@gmail.com / senlibraire@gmail.com
www.harmattansenegal.com

L'HARMATTAN BÉNIN
ISOR-BENIN
01 BP 359 COTONOU-RP
Quartier Gbèdjromèdé,
Rue Agbélenco, Lot 1247 I
Tél : 00 229 21 32 53 79
christian_dablaka123@yahoo.fr

Achevé d'imprimer par Corlet Numérique - 14110 Condé-sur-Noireau
N° d'Imprimeur : 130104 - Dépôt légal : juin 2016 - *Imprimé en France*